THE TWO
Elizabeths

ALSO BY VIRGINIA WEIR

Stay a Friend as Long as You Can, A Memoir

Rite of Spring, A Novel

ISBN 978-1-7359490-1-7

THE TWO
Elizabeths

A Novella

Virginia Weir

for Paul

Table of Contents

Prologue

The Time Log

If Liz did not improve her work performance, and soon, Elizabeth would have to let her go. It would be difficult—in general, a mess—and certainly Elizabeth didn't *want* to let her go, but the record she had been keeping for the past two weeks did not lie. It was a log of Liz's time—blocks of four lines with a fifth crossing over them, like a sketch of a little picket fence across the white page. Each time Liz got up and left from her desk, Elizabeth made a mark. At first she had kept the log locked in her top side drawer, but then through the side door to the reception area she would see Liz leave again, and she'd have to unlock the drawer to make a mark, so she now kept it in a folder on her desk, taking care to lock it if she went to the Ladies Room or to lunch.

There was plenty of work to be done. They had been notified of several new applications from the National Science Foundation, but Liz had not yet investigated any of them. She hadn't seen the grants calendar Liz had told her would be done last week, either. Liz would be at her desk, then away, then back for a moment or two, then away. Elizabeth knew there was very little that Liz did in the context of her job that would require such constant up-and-down. Occasional copying and scanning, and that was it.

Elizabeth didn't *like* keeping the Log. It made her uncomfortable. And keeping track of Liz's movements was actually taking up a good part of her own day. It would be a lot easier if Liz's performance assessment were coming up; she could integrate the current difficulties into the evaluation and if it came to letting her go, she'd have a well documented back-up. As it was, her evaluation four months previous had been generally outstanding. Elizabeth now regretted some of her more enthusiastic comments about Liz's work: *"Ms. MacKenzie is able to prioritize amongst competing office needs and uses time efficiently to produce highly professional work in a timely manner... Ms. MacKenzie's excellent computer skills have made her a valuable resource in designing various tracking systems to manage office information and grant reporting requirements... Ms. MacKenzie would be difficult to replace..."*

How could someone change so quickly?

Elizabeth sighed and looked out the giant window overlooking the parking lot and a bank of Norwegian pines that obscured the view of the next industrial park down the road. She wished, again, that they had never had to move from their cozy one-room office on campus to this spacious, modern office building off-campus with the rest of Institutional Advancement. They had bothered no one in that domain, and no one had bothered them. Her contact with the vice president, Don Lindell (the latest in a series over the 20 years she'd been at the college), had been minimal and often conducted through interoffice mail. She had liked it that way. Now, there were weekly meetings accomplishing nothing (she had more experience, and certainly more common sense in her little finger than anyone at those meetings), and Elizabeth suspected that now Liz spent much of her time away from her desk socializing with the other staff—most of them Lindell's new hires—young, ambitious, career-types.

Tom Murphy, for one. Thirty-ish, having spent five years in the insurance business, he looked pleasant and harmless in his gray conservative suits and wire frame glasses. But she had seen him joking recently with Liz at the copier, and the two of them had stopped suddenly when they saw her. Murphy had boldly said to her, "Good morning, Elizabeth," in an insincere voice.

Ann Lupinsky was another bad influence, Elizabeth thought. Ann, who had been in banking and was trying the non-profit world of academia, was blonde and petite, well-made-up and perfectly professional with her trim-fitting suits and two-inch heels. She had seen Liz in Ann's office, supposedly to retrieve some statistics on last year's Annual Fund, sitting in front of Ann's desk talking quite earnestly about something that was obviously not the Annual Fund. Ann was 33, the same age as Liz, and so perhaps Liz was feeling that she wanted to be more like Ann. Perhaps Liz was now looking to Ann as a role model. They each had children, but other than that they were worlds apart. Elizabeth had seen through Ann from the moment Lindell hired her. A ladder-climber, a quick-study. She had seen probably 20 of them come and go in Development over the years.

Liz was not like Ann. She was simpler, more natural. She didn't have the capacity to glad-hand. It was a quality that Elizabeth had appreciated in her. Last week, Liz had come in wearing a purple suit. Elizabeth complimented her on it, although personally she thought it too short and ridiculously overdressed for an assistant. "Oh, I got it at the consignment shop," Liz had said, blushing. They hadn't been talking as much as they used to. In the old days, Liz would have come in and dramatically modeled the new suit, making her laugh, even, and asking her opinion. But not anymore.

In their old office, it had just been the two of them. "The two Elizabeths," she had once heard someone joke, perhaps in a not-friendly way, but she hadn't minded. She had liked being the two Elizabeths, although in the office Liz went by "Liz" to avoid confusion between the two of them. A few times Liz's husband, Jack, had been put through the office receptionist to Elizabeth, having forgotten to ask for "Liz" instead of "Elizabeth." They had laughed about it.

They had laughed about a lot of things. She had looked forward to the afternoons when Liz would trade the baby with Jack and come in to work. She liked even better the days when Liz had to bring the baby in for the trade-off because Jack was late. Elizabeth felt the arrangement was rather flexible and supportive of Liz, since work time was undeniably taken up by these transfers. The baby, Isabel, was a good baby, with the deepest blue eyes Elizabeth had ever seen. Liz would say, "Say hi to Elizabeth," and Isabel would smile, and Liz would hand the baby over to her and it was all Elizabeth could do to keep from smothering the child in kisses, she was so beautiful. But she restrained herself.

Now that Liz was working full-time, Isabel was in daycare and rarely came to the office. At a year old, Elizabeth thought, the baby was probably able to handle the long hours of daycare. Liz left every evening at 5 on the dot, and while Elizabeth could appreciate that Liz wanted to be with her baby, she still found it somehow annoying. There had been a few times when she had been out of the office when Liz actually left around 4:45. She had called in and the receptionist said Liz had already left. Elizabeth had not mentioned this to Liz. She suspected it was happening each time she was out of the office at the end of the day.

"Don't you ever get *bored* working all the time, in the same place, at the same job?" Liz had asked her, a few months ago, soon after she had begun working full-time in her position. There was a tone of flippancy, almost buoyancy, in her voice.

"No. I am always able to find something that interests me, something I want to pursue." The smile on Liz's face had faded. Elizabeth hadn't meant to sound quite so stern, so she said, "Of *course* there are slow times...."

"Don't you ever just long for a vacation, a long one? You get a lot of time each year since you've been here so long; you could probably actually take one."

For some reason this question had irritated Elizabeth and she had chosen not to answer, just smiling briefly and closing the door between their two offices with the comment that she had some notes to prepare for Dr. Patel's grant report to the National Science Foundation.

Elizabeth knew exactly how much vacation she had accumulated: six weeks and three days, and another six weeks accumulating for this year. Six weeks was a lot of time, and she wished that she could simply be reimbursed for vacation. The college allowed employees to carry over one year's worth of vacation, and she had barely managed to use what she had last year and get a special dispensation for the other days. She and her mother had gone to New Hampshire for four days. The other five weeks had been used here and there, having the house painted, getting new carpeting installed, shopping for fabric for a new bed canopy and matching drapes. She'd also taken additional ice skating lessons. There was not another way she would have spent her vacation, but it wasn't exactly like a vacation. Queries from colleagues about it irritated her. Revealing the fact that she stayed home was like some kind of *faux pas*, and it was ridiculous. Some people, obviously, did not have the responsibility of an elderly mother and an old house.

Elizabeth was aware that Liz knew she would like to take a vacation away somewhere. Liz also knew that Elizabeth was often bored—by her life with her mother in the house where she grew up in Milport, by college life and politics, by the drive to campus every day. (That first week after they had moved to the industrial offices with the rest of Institutional Advancement, Elizabeth had twice driven to the main campus out of habit. She hoped no one had recognized her car pulling into and out of the parking lot.) And so she resented this outright question, *Don't you ever want to take a long vacation?*

What? she thought now, and leave you here to gossip all day and get nothing done? Definitely not.

That thought was, perhaps, unfair. She had thought of really going away this year, on her own, on a tour or a cruise, perhaps. But she couldn't really consider it until this business with Liz was settled. Liz was going to have to decide if she wanted to stay in the Grants Office (as far as Elizabeth knew, there weren't any other assistant positions open), and if she did, more concentration to the tasks at hand would be required.

Hints had been given, without any specific reprimand. "Liz, this *Update* is missing page numbers. You need to spend a little more time proofing before you distribute it." "Liz, did you pick up those samples from Dr. Patel? He's waiting for them." She did not appreciate devising these tasks for her. Liz was a mature woman; Elizabeth had seen a lot of that maturity when Liz first started working at the college; it was why she'd gone way out of her way to get her hired from the temporary agency.

And so Elizabeth decided she would speak to her, informally, one last time, and be as direct as she felt it was her responsibility to be. She waited until it was around 4:30. The mid-summer sky was still bright; there were several daylight hours left. She took an article on teen pregnancy that she had been reading into Liz's area under the pretense of filing it in the Information files.

"Do we have a file on teen pregnancy?" Elizabeth asked. (She liked paper files—never mind the "green" efforts on campus. Although she no longer felt it necessary to keep blank application forms from previous years, it gave her a sense of readiness to have the latest hard-copy applications in the file drawer, in original print and color, no pages missing, for reference.) It occurred to Elizabeth that there was no one in the Sociology Department who would be available (or probably capable) of working on a proposal about teen pregnancy, but one never knew. If she applied for an Upward Bound program grant, the statistics or a quote might be handy, and it would be there, in the file.

Liz squinted, then shrugged. "I don't think so."

Elizabeth bent over and pulled out the drawer marked: *Information P-Z*. There was no file, either under "Teens" or "Pregnancy". She decided not to bring that up right now. And, sensing a tension from Liz, she decided not to ask her to type a label for a file just now, either.

"You know," Elizabeth said, finally, "things haven't been the same since we moved off-campus."

7

"No," Liz said, reluctant, busying herself with something in her pocketbook, but obviously waiting to hear what Elizabeth would say next.

Let me just say it, she thought.

"You're socializing a lot, Liz, and I see things falling apart around here." There, it was said. She glanced around the reception area, which included Liz's desk and computer and the twelve file cabinets, both vertical and horizontal, full of information, applications, and copies of actual grant proposals. Elizabeth wished, as she said it, that she had phrased it somehow differently, as nothing in Liz's area looked particularly messy, but she knew things weren't getting done.

Liz's face was paler than normal, but she faced her as she said, carefully, "Elizabeth, there's not all that much to do."

"What about those tables of contents? Are they all cross-referenced with the appropriate departments? Each issue of those magazines has something that might be of potential interest to the faculty."

"I mean something *challenging*. You know, if I could have something new and different to do—something of my own—or even something for the others." Liz's face was filling with color now, and her speech picked up. "Tom needs some database help, and Ann wanted me to proof a couple of the appeal letters she was sending out...."

So it was as she had suspected. Tom and Ann were trying to borrow her employee.

"Liz," she said, and paused, and sighed, lightly. "If I can't depend on you to take care of tasks that, while I admit are not the most exciting in the world, are still very important to our function as a department," she here avoided the word *trust,* "how could I depend on you to carry out more challenging jobs? There is plenty to be done—plenty we *could* do—but only if our administrative tasks are under control."

Liz's face had paled again, and Elizabeth knew she had made her angry. That wasn't what she had wanted. But couldn't Liz understand her frustration? Every other department on campus had a full-time assistant. She was one of only three female directors at the college, and she had struggled for upwards of ten years to get the budget for a full-time person; now she finally had it, and the work wasn't getting done. It rankled her.

"Look," Elizabeth said, "I just want you to think about how it's been. Think about how things have changed, and how they could change. And if you're committed to working on it with me, we'll go on and look at possibilities."

Liz had looked down at her desk and nodded.

"Let's talk about it. It's Monday today. Let's talk on Friday. Okay?"

Liz nodded again.

Later, in her office, Elizabeth felt good about the way she had handled the issue overall. Not too harshly. After all, Liz was by far the best assistant she'd had. That evening, Elizabeth composed a brief email to both Tom and Ann, with a cc to Lindell, stating in a clear but not unpleasant way that while she would be glad to be able to offer the help of her assistant on their work, there were projects in the Grants area that were ongoing and time-consuming, and Liz would not be available to assist them.

Chapter 1

A Temporary Assistant

The news of her aunt's death was not unexpected, but still Elizabeth felt her eyes well up with tears. If she had been alone in the office, she might have cried outright; instead, she retrieved the box of tissues from her drawer and blew her nose. Other than the hum of the computers, the room was quiet, and Elizabeth knew she was being observed.

"Are you okay?" the new assistant asked.

"Yes, yes. I just had news that my aunt died. This morning."

The assistant was quiet for a couple of moments and then said, "It's always a surprise." There was a calmness in her voice that somehow made Elizabeth feel better.

The new assistant's name was also Elizabeth—Elizabeth MacKenzie. The temp agency had sent her over to the college just this morning, the third in as many weeks after Elizabeth was dissatisfied with each. She had been without regular help for almost six months, and she was trying to force John Ackerman, Director of Human Resources (and a complete wimp, as far as Elizabeth was concerned) to find someone appropriate to fill the position.

Elizabeth sighed, shakily. "It *is* a surprise. I just saw her last night at the nursing home. She seemed weak, but she was talking...." She sighed again. Aunt May's 85-year-old face, with its soft, jowly white skin and hard blue eyes, was still fresh in her mind. There would be a lot of preparation to do for the funeral, and it would probably all be up to her. God knows, her brother Tom was useless for anything domestic. She called her mother to tell her Aunt May was dead.

"She's gone. 8:20 a.m., they said."

"Well," was all her mother said. "Will you come home early?"

"I'll come home at lunchtime."

"Is there anything I can do to help you?" Elizabeth MacKenzie asked when she got off the phone. Elizabeth liked this girl. She was distant, but polite and responsive at the same time. She dressed a bit casually, perhaps, in slacks and a cotton sweater, but her clothes were pressed and not gaudy.

"Yes," she said. "There is." On the table in the cramped room were three, foot-high piles of mail from the past month that needed sorting. Elizabeth had had a horrible time getting the past two temps to understand how she wanted the mail sorted: grant information and applications from federal agencies, separate from private foundations; interoffice mail; outside mail; and "other." All one had to do was quickly skim the nature of the item and put it in a pile, she explained.

The other Elizabeth smiled. "Would you like me to make files for these?"

"I *would* really appreciate it if you would file the applications. And, if you have time, go through the file drawers for really old applications. We can toss those."

Elizabeth then showed her the tiny side room, lit by one overhead bulb, which housed the twelve file cabinets. "My God!" the new Elizabeth exclaimed. "I hope the foundation under this room is solid."

"Well, the college assigns space, and I do what I can with it," Elizabeth said. She was actually quite proud of the tight configuration. "Even in the digital age, there is a lot of paperwork in grant-writing; a lot of forms and applications, and a lot of information-gathering."

"I can imagine."

"If you can manage the mail, and if you could go through the CDs and see what's on them and print a directory, I would be very grateful. I've had no chance to get caught up, and I honestly don't know how long I'll be out. Probably all week." Elizabeth examined the other Elizabeth. She was a bit taller than herself, with short, curly brown hair. Her face was plain; she had a quick, pleasant smile, but she was not an obsequious type. Elizabeth realized she was feeling hopeful. If this girl could work well on her own, perhaps she would be interested in a regular job.

She also realized that in the past two hours, she had almost forgotten about her aunt. A wave of sadness came over her again, but this time it was accompanied by a feeling of challenge: work to be done, whether she liked it or not, so she may as well get to it.

The phone rang. It was Sahil Patel, who called Elizabeth at least twice a day (more when they were working on a grant proposal), and she told him the news. "I am very sorry to hear that," Sahil said, formally. "You will be out all week?"

"Probably."

"Ah, well. May I call you at home, as to the sending of flowers?"

"There's no need, but you can call, if you like."

"I will."

"I have an assistant, for the time being. Her name is Elizabeth MacKenzie."

"Two Elizabeth's," Sahil chuckled.

Elizabeth ignored him. "You can speak to her if you need anything in the office."

When she got off, the phone rang again. Her mother told her it was almost noon; was she coming home?

Elizabeth gathered her things. It was good that there was nothing major pending this week. "I'll give you my home phone number in Milport, in case there is any emergency. Please don't give it out. Just take a message. I will call in. And please let people know, discreetly, what has happened. It will save me a lot of explanation." The other Elizabeth nodded, quite calm. Elizabeth supposed she ought to call Lindell, but she didn't want to. "Also, please call Dr. Lindell's office—the number is on that roster—and explain who you are and what has happened. He's the vice president of Institutional Advancement. They're in an office off-campus."

"I will."

"Are you called by any other name?" Elizabeth asked.

"Excuse me?" The other Elizabeth looked puzzled.

"I was only thinking that it is a bit awkward to have two people in an office and both have the same name. Do you ever go by a nickname? Beth, or Liz, or something else?"

"My sisters call me Liz."

"May I call you that?"

The other Elizabeth blushed, hesitant. "I guess so. Sure."

"Thank you for your help, Liz."

"You're welcome. Good luck with the funeral and all."

Chapter 2

Aunt May's Funeral

Aunt May's funeral went as smoothly as could be expected, with three cousins coming in from Ohio and staying at the house. Why they couldn't see the comfort and privacy of staying in a motel, Elizabeth would never understand, but her mother seemed to enjoy the company. The preparations were standard; the Russian Orthodox service was long and formal, and Aunt May was buried in the plot she had purchased shortly after she had moved to Bridgewater. Elizabeth called in every day, at various times, and received a positive report with each call. Several people from the college had sent her condolence notes, so they must have gotten the information from Liz. She found out that Lindell's office had distributed a memo about the death. It was strange how people you barely spoke to in the hallways felt they should send condolences for a distant relative, and then, probably, go back to not speaking to you. Part of the gossipy nature of academia, Elizabeth thought—everyone loves a drama. And death—even of someone you don't know or care about—is a drama. She didn't like to admit it, but she enjoyed getting the notes: *"Dr. Elizabeth Wright and Family."*

"I didn't know you were a doctor," her cousin Edward commented, looking over her shoulder. Elizabeth didn't know him, or care to know him. He was her father's brother's son, quite a bit younger than herself.

Elizabeth smiled primly at him and took the note into the other room to read, not bothering to explain that her degree was an "Ed.D.", a doctorate in Education in her field— marine biology. The two-year course was much shorter than a regular doctorate, and no thesis was required. For a few years she had felt vaguely apologetic when someone called her "Dr. Wright," but she had grown used to it; it was not a lie, after all, it *was* the title of her degree.

Most of the notes were brief: *"Elizabeth, sorry to hear about your loss",* etc. She liked Sahil's note the best. *"Hope you are feeling well with all your family there. When you get back I need to talk to you right away."* He had sent an elaborate arrangement of flowers. He knew quite well that she would be very glad when her family was not there anymore, and she appreciated the fact that he was honest about his focus, which was to get this latest application out by the end of the month. She could always count on Sahil to be exactly who he was.

The funeral was on Thursday, and the cousins piled into their SUV for the drive back to Ohio on Friday morning. Elizabeth was exhausted. She plopped down in front of the television, and let her mother clean around her. She knew her mother would work all day, stripping all sheets and dusting every corner. She could clean for hours without speaking, just an occasional humming, quickly stifled by a change in task, and that was the agenda for today. At noon, Elizabeth called the office. Liz professed to have everything under control. Elizabeth found herself giving Liz a description of the funeral. Liz was easy to talk to.

"You must be relieved that you have your house back to yourself," Liz said. Elizabeth watched her mother, on her knees vacuuming under the couch.

"Yes, we're both somewhat relieved."

"Both?"

"Mother and I."

"Oh, I was confused."

"My mother lives with me." Elizabeth took the phone back into the kitchen. "So," she continued, "did you print out directories?"

"Yes, no problem. I also thought of a way you might be able to organize your proposals. But I didn't want to go on with it without talking to you about it."

"Sounds interesting." Elizabeth liked this girl. "Did the agency tell you I would need you for a few weeks?"

"Yes."

"Did they tell you it was a temporary-to-permanent job?"

Liz laughed. "You mean a 'lease-to-own'? Yes, actually, they did."

"Well, good. I'll see you Monday, then."

"Monday."

After she got off the phone with Liz, she called Marjorie Harding, her contact in Admissions across the hall, and asked Marjorie whether she'd seen the new girl and what she thought.

"Oh, yes, I've seen her. I wondered who she was. She seems very.... efficient. Friendly. She came in here asking whether we had any large garbage bags—I did, and I gave her a box, and she said she'd pay me back—and I went in later, you know, just to say hello—that office could be so lonely, I was thinking—and she had the place upside-down—all kinds of stuff. She said you'd said to clean the files if she had a chance. Well, I guess she had a chance. She asked me who to call to haul the stuff away, and I gave her the Maintenance number. You want me to check on her again? This morning she brought me in a new box of bags. Must've bought them herself."

Marjorie could chat one's ears off. Elizabeth was a little worried about the volume of stuff it sounded like Liz was disposing of, but she was also very tired. She positioned herself in front of the television again with a sandwich left over from the funeral. When the sun went down, her mother asked her if she minded if they didn't have a regular meal.

"Oh, Mother, sit down and relax. Please." She got up and made her mother a sandwich and they watched ice skating semi-finals. Elizabeth had cancelled her lesson this week.

"Now that's a pretty costume," Mrs. Wright said of the Russian skater wearing a traditional white leotard and simple skirt. Elizabeth preferred the emerald-green sequins of the previous skater.

They watched for another half-hour in silence. In the twilight the unlit room had a golden glow. Elizabeth closed her eyes for a while. She enjoyed the clean furniture and the faint smell of lemon from her mother's polish. When she opened her eyes she saw that her mother was silently crying. Mrs. Wright dabbed her eyes. "I'm tired," she said. "She wasn't herself in that nursing home. I miss her," she added, a moment later.

"I know you do," Elizabeth said, and patted her mother's hand. Tomorrow they could go back to their routine and things would get back to normal.

Chapter 3

A Permanent Assistant

The small office was as airy and clean as Elizabeth had ever seen it when she returned on Monday. She was about half an hour late, taking her time, and when she arrived Liz was in front of the computer, clicking away as though she'd worked there forever. For a moment, Elizabeth felt disoriented. All the books and binders behind her desk were dusted and met the edge of the bookcase. There even appeared to be extra room on some of the shelves. This meant Liz had tossed some things, which made Elizabeth a bit nervous; she hadn't expected her to do so much. Along the other shelves of periodicals that formed a freestanding wall against her desk—Elizabeth liked to think of it as her "library"—each magazine holder with a laser-printed label identifying its contents. The piles of mail on the table had disappeared, and both the table and her large desk appeared to be polished.

"Good morning," Liz said, smiling.

"Well, good morning. You certainly did some work last week."

"I like to put things in order."

"Well, I thank you for it. The office looks very nice."

Pink message slips from her voice mail were arranged in a cascading order, on top of some printouts. Most of them were from Sahil, and Elizabeth crumpled and tossed them. She'd told him she'd call him and she would. Of course, Liz didn't know any better than to write down each call. Under the slips were printouts that appeared to be some kind of database fields.

"What's this?" she asked.

"Oh, well, from what I could see in the files it seemed like you could use some kind of database to track your grants."

Elizabeth had been doing just that, on aging index cards. "You know how to do that on the computer?" she asked.

Liz shrugged. "Pretty much. It's no big deal."

They defined the database fields, and Elizabeth gave her permission to set about creating the database. After that, she was on the phone the rest of the morning, returning calls, going over the story of the funeral, thanking people for their cards, etcetera. The day passed quickly; Elizabeth was pleased at a sense of production that she hadn't had in a while, and knew it was due mostly to Liz being so efficient and easy to be around. It was a small office, after all, and Elizabeth had felt comfortable making phone calls that would be overheard.

By the end of the week, she had found out that Liz was 30, as she had suspected; she was married to a man named Jack who worked in an auto repair shop; she had a son who was 5. Her previous jobs had been as an assistant; she had a bachelor's degree in communications but no particular career goals. She had a young child, so this was understandable. Liz seemed a decent sort of person, and Elizabeth knew she wanted to hire her.

She called John Ackerman in Human Resources from an office across the hall so that Liz wouldn't be forced to overhear a conversation about her. "You want her, you got her," said Ackerman, "but there's only budget for half-time."

"Would she get benefits?"

"We might be able to work something out. Get a copy of her resume."

"I'll get back to you."

Before Liz left that afternoon, Elizabeth put forth her proposal. "As you might have gathered, Liz," she said, formally, "I am very pleased with your performance in the Grants Office, and I would like to offer you the job. However, at this time I can only offer a part-time position— although we may be able to work something out regarding benefits."

"That sounds perfect," Liz said, smiling. Her face fell slightly. "But there's something I have to tell you."

Elizabeth felt her jaw tighten.

i"I'm trying—*we're* trying—to get pregnant again. But I am still going to have to work no matter what. After the baby comes, too. That's why a part-time job would be perfect."

"Are you pregnant now?"

"No."

"Did you have trouble with your other pregnancy?"
Liz smiled proudly. "No. I worked right up to the end and came back after six weeks. Part-time, that is."

"I don't see a problem."

The fact was, she was touched by Liz's honesty. Liz had been under no obligation to tell her of her personal intentions, but in truth she would have been annoyed if Liz had become pregnant within a few months of being hired. Of course things could change; they could always change. Elizabeth was pleasantly surprised to find herself trusting Liz and looking forward to working with her.

After Liz had gone, Elizabeth called John Ackerman again to tell him to investigate the benefits of a part-time position.

Despite the fact that she was happy with the arrangement (perhaps Liz wouldn't have been able to accept a full-time position), she couldn't resist niggling Ackerman.

"John, just tell me, will I ever have the budget for a full-time assistant? I'm a one-person office; proportionately I bring in a huge portion of the college's income and I can't even get an assistant full-time."

She could almost hear him shrugging. She knew that, like many in Administration, Ackerman did not like her. Mostly, they were a lazy, unprofessional bunch over there. And while she had to be careful who she spoke to, her mind remained unchanged. Life was too short (her mind drifted briefly to her aunt's face in the casket last week) to worry about whether people liked her or not.

Chapter 4

Other Assistants

Liz talked freely about herself, but she wasn't a chatterbox like Charlene, the assistant-before-last. Charlene could talk non-stop literally for an hour until Elizabeth thought she might scream. Instead, she would say quietly, "Well, now, Charlene, I have work to do and I'm sure you do, too." Charlene would blush and stammer a bit, and go back to her computer screen, or open and shut file drawers, but like clockwork within an hour she'd be talking again. Elizabeth couldn't even remember what it was she talked about. It was very frustrating.

Debbie, the girl after Charlene, had been a temp-to-perm and in contrast to Charlene she hardly ever talked, except, it seemed, when Elizabeth was out of the office—and then she did nothing *but* talk. She would apparently be on the phone all day and sometimes neglected to pick up incoming calls. Sahil said he had tried to reach Elizabeth one day for over an hour. Finally he had driven across campus. Debbie was on the phone and had the audacity to remain on the phone for another full minute while he waited. When she came back the next day, Elizabeth listened with patience to Sahil's complaining on the phone, looking at Debbie's back as she typed the narrative to his grant. Elizabeth was peeved, but decided not to speak to Debbie about it. The fact was, she was so uncomfortable with Debbie's day-long silences that she was going to let her go. Since it was temp-to-perm, no explanations were necessary.

On Friday morning of that week she told Debbie, "We won't be needing you to come back on Monday."

"Why?" Debbie's voice was bluntly suspicious.

Elizabeth felt flustered but recovered herself. "Well, frankly, I don't think it's a good fit. I need someone who is more interactive, who can be both assertive and polite with faculty..."

"It's that Patel guy, isn't it. He told you I was on the phone, didn't he. Well, my brother got beat up last week. I had to be on the phone."

This was a bald-faced lie, confirming her decision. "Well, I'm sorry about your brother; you should have told me. I hope he's okay."

"You change your mind?"

"No." They were standing across the room from each other.

"You don't know shit about my life."

"No, I don't." She did not need to add the refrain, *and I don't want to.* Elizabeth was about to tell her she could go now and she would sign off for the unworked hours today, but she didn't need to. Debbie picked up her things and dropped her timeslip on Elizabeth's desk. She waited, hugging her handbag until Elizabeth signed it, and then left without another word.

Elizabeth had sat back down in the quiet office, relieved and perspiring slightly. Other peoples' lives were not her fault; it was just not a good fit.

Chapter 5

"I've Got News"

"I've got news," was how Liz announced that she was pregnant. Her face was clear and faintly rosy, Elizabeth noted. She was just barely along; the baby was not due until January. "You're the first person I've told—outside of Jack, of course," Liz said, making eye contact with her for the first time.

Liz had warned her she was intending this, and now it had come to pass. Obviously, Liz wanted to know she approved, that this was okay, that Elizabeth would not hold it against her that she was pregnant. Realizing this, Elizabeth could not understand why she was vaguely annoyed at the news. Perhaps it was because the official permanent part-time position had only begun two weeks ago, after much additional red tape with the temporary agency over Liz's hiring. Elizabeth had spared Liz the details. And now, just as she had a permanent assistant, the future of the office seemed shaky again.

"You've been to your doctor?" She had a vague recollection that it took eight weeks to be sure, but of course that didn't make sense, especially if Liz had been trying to get pregnant.

Liz nodded.

"Well, that's wonderful news," she said, somewhat mechanically. "I'm very happy for you."

Liz didn't appear to notice her reserve. "Jack would like another boy. I'd like a girl, of course," she said, trying not to smile too broadly and failing.

"I agree with you. Boys are... well, *boys.*"

Liz laughed. "Yeah. You can say that again. You should see Tyler running around the house." She paused, considering something. "You know, we should have you over to dinner one of these days."

Elizabeth smiled politely. She was curious about Liz's home life, but not sure whether she wanted to spend an entire evening with them.

"There goes another one," her mother said that evening when Elizabeth told her that Liz was pregnant.

"I don't know, Mother. She *said* she had to work."

"That's baloney. With two young children? What does her husband do? Can't he support them?"

Elizabeth did not reply. She was sorry she'd said anything to her mother.

That night, she had a dream in which she was talking to Liz. It was just regular conversation, about nothing important. Then, as they talked, a window began to slide down between them—a very thin window, with four panes. Liz appeared not to notice and continued talking. Elizabeth could read her lips: *I've got news.*

She remembered the dream at breakfast as she sipped her coffee and had a small bowl of oatmeal. The window in her mother's bedroom had to be replaced. She would take care of it one of these weekends.

"Working in the afternoons works out good for me," Liz said. "I can get over my morning sickness." She chuckled.

Elizabeth noticed she was laughing a lot these days. "I'm a little silly, I know," Liz said.

Elizabeth smiled at her. In spite of her worries, everything seemed to be flowing smoothly. A month had passed and Liz showed up, on time, each day for work and except for occasional nausea she seemed like herself. She had finished entering all the grant information into a database, created a report that listed the submission and receipt dates of various proposals, and offered to help write a grant. She assured Elizabeth she needed to work at least part-time after the baby came. "We'll talk about that closer to your due date," Elizabeth said, but she began to feel hopeful.

She even began to be curious about the baby. She imagined it as a happy child, a girl, with light brown hair. A quiet, intelligent child.

Chapter 6

Dr. Patel

"You know," Liz said one day a few weeks after she began working as a permanent assistant, "I think Dr. Patel has a crush on you. He calls all the time."

Elizabeth had her back to Liz, filing a newsletter from the Association of Fundraising Professionals. She could have had Liz do this, but she didn't like people working behind her. She didn't answer Liz. The silence grew so long that she knew Liz believed she hadn't heard the question and thought better of asking again.

"You're wrong," she said, somewhat bluntly, keeping her back to Liz. "Dr. Patel is married and has two little girls."

"Oh," Liz said brightly.

The fact was, Elizabeth had noticed a growing attentiveness from Sahil. They had worked together on various grants for fifteen years now (she had become practically an expert in the workings of the National Science Foundation), but over the past year Sahil had become more casual, staying later, ordering Chinese on the nights where there was a deadline. It wasn't as though he was working; he just sat with her and read this section or that of the narrative. She decided to use these last-minute evenings as her uninterrupted chance to get the budget numbers right, since Sahil was in such a rush during the day.

Last week they had finished a grant requesting more spectometry equipment for the science lab. Liz had stayed the whole day, until 6, typing and editing the revised sections Elizabeth handed her. Sahil had come in with Chinese just before Liz left, and had stayed until the grant was finished, around 9.

At one point Elizabeth had looked up to find him looking at her. It wasn't a stare; it was more of an uninterrupted gaze. "You are so resourceful, Elizabeth," he said.

For a second, she was embarrassed and her heart throbbed in her throat; then the feeling cleared. "Well, thank you, Sahil," she said, somewhat sarcastically, and laughed.

This grant required a printed copy. They finished it, and Sahil helped copy and package it for FedEx. He would take it to the latest drop-off nearby site. In the dark parking lot, he walked Elizabeth to her car. "Good night," he said and touched her shoulder lightly. "I will see you tomorrow." Across the lot in his car, he waited until she had warmed up her car and pulled out before he left.

Elizabeth thought about Sahil as she drove the familiar back streets to her house. She liked these courtesies of his, performed without discussion or irony—almost without thought. He was a professional, and gentlemanly. She wished, perhaps, that he took better care of his physical self; he was always eating in a rush, usually fast food like the Chinese they'd had tonight, and he was getting a gut. Otherwise, he was a reasonably attractive man. He was as tall and as she was, and the same age—50—with thick, wavy hair that was still all black. Sahil's wife, Juliette, was a medical doctor and was gone many evenings. Elizabeth had met her once at a faculty party—a thin, unattractive, French woman who was quite a bit younger than him. They had married late and had two children who were cared for by a nanny when Sahil also had to work late.

Elizabeth imagined, briefly, inviting him to dinner at her house, but realized she would not want her mother at home if Sahil should come over. This thought made her realize that perhaps she wasn't thinking as straightforwardly about Sahil as she should be.

She pulled into her driveway and sat for a few moments. It was only a little after 9, but she was very tired. Was Sahil thinking about her? She thought of him looking at her tonight, and his comment, *You are so resourceful, Elizabeth.* An image from "Beauty and the Beast" came to mind: Catherine on her balcony above the dangerous city, wearing a long white dressing gown billowing gently in the breeze, observed by Vincent with desire—and real affection, of course.

Through the crack in the window she could smell grass from the neighbor's yard. It was warm for April. The porch light went on suddenly and Elizabeth saw her mother squinting from behind the living room curtain, and she knew she had better go in.

Chapter 7

A Bad Experience

It was not as though Elizabeth was totally inexperienced in sexual matters. Sex was messy and complicated at best and she had decided early on not to bother with it. She wasn't the child-raising type; her education and a career had always been important to her, and she didn't see where marriage would fit in. And in the last 10 years she'd had her mother to consider. It wasn't that she didn't sometimes yearn for companionship and a bit of affection, but that never seemed possible. The world of intimacy—that kind of intimacy—was an all-or-nothing world.

When she was just 27, in graduate school at the university nearby, she worked for a pittance on a biology project. Elizabeth and a group of five other graduate students had taken turns monitoring plankton counts. She would not forget the project: "The influence of nutrient load on plankton population in freshwater ponds." She was almost done with her coursework by that time and was taking only one education class at night, along with 12 hours a week in the small trailer set up on the edge of a city park. It was a somewhat lonely six months there, but Elizabeth was used to being alone and came to like studying specimens and writing up reports in the little trailer, the bustle of the city just outside the thin metal shell. It somehow felt less strange than her tiny student-housing apartment half a mile away.

She remembered pretending not to remember Mike's name the first few times they worked together. She didn't know why she did this, perhaps just to prove to herself her disinterest in him. Michael Dalalian. He was tall and thin and somewhat scruffy looking, but his face was square and clean-cut no matter how long he went without combing his hair. They were two months into the project and Mike was new to the team. Elizabeth was assigned to work with him, and they were together every morning for six weeks. After so much solitude in the small space, it was awkward to share it with a large man, but he was quiet and intelligent and easy-going, and Elizabeth liked him from the start. She found herself putting on just a touch of lipstick in the morning.

"Are you wearing lipstick?" he asked.

She rubbed her lips together and did not reply. After that, she dispensed with the lipstick. She wanted him to notice her, but not *notice* her. She didn't know what she wanted, except that she thought about him more and more on the afternoons when they weren't together in the lab. Finally, close to the end of the project, Elizabeth invited Michael to dinner at her apartment.

"A home-cooked meal!" he'd exclaimed, with a touch of sarcasm that she appreciated.

He arrived at her apartment fifteen minutes late. Elizabeth had been quite nervous about the dinner, which was somewhat traditional: baked chicken and potatoes and a salad. She had even bought a bottle of wine. Michael had also brought wine. All the ease they had developed in the tiny trailer disappeared in her apartment. Throughout dinner she was uncomfortable, suddenly noticing the shabbiness of her place. While they ate, the bed with its white quilt waited in the corner of the room like some kind of animal while they ate. There was no place to sit except at the table or on the bed.

Michael filled in all the awkward silences, trying hard to act comfortable. After dinner, he opened the second bottle of wine and sat down on the edge of the bed. He was talking about music, how one band was better than another and lamenting the fact that she didn't even have a stereo. She washed the dishes. Finally, he said, "Elizabeth, come here."

She went to him in a daze, inebriated by the wine, and he pulled her easily onto his lap. Then he kissed her, hungrily. It was very rough and surprising, Michael's tongue in her mouth, and she didn't know if she liked it. She remembered thinking, *Do I like this?* and thinking, in spite of her inebriation, that if she was thinking about it she probably didn't. He leaned back with her very gracefully onto the bed, and his hand went to her breast with a sort of massage to discover what was there. She let him do this for a moment, and then he moved his hand under her blouse to her back and unhooked her bra, again so gracefully that she began to think of how many times he had done this before. Many times, obviously. And when the flesh of his hand met her breast, she startled and pushed it away. He mistook her gesture for one of desire, and his hand went to her jeans and was in her underwear so fast that she hardly knew what had happened until he was fingering her and she exclaimed, "No!"

Michael was drunk. She remembered the dazed look on his face as he pulled back from her, squinting slightly in the still bright room.

"No," he repeated, confused.

"No." Elizabeth, sitting up, wanted badly to reach under her blouse and rehook her bra, but did not want the embarrassment of doing it in front of him. How would she get him out of her apartment? Was there any way to retreat gracefully?

Michael had laid back dramatically on her bed, his arm over his forehead as though he had a headache. They remained in their positions for over a minute and finally he spoke, without removing his arm. "Three months of little touches in tight spaces, little bumps there, little teases everywhere. A mind like steel trap. An attractive, trim body. I think I'm dealing with the most mysteriously straight, intriguing woman. A whole new—hey, maybe a whole old—way of flirting. I'm game. I'm interested. She invites me to her place." Michael had rolled over on his side on the bed, propped up with one arm. "And I think, wow, great, finally. The mystery deepens. She's as stiff as ever, but that's part of the mystery. I think she knows what she wants and has her own way of getting it."

He was waiting now for her to say something, but Elizabeth remained sitting on the bed, unmovable.

"You're a virgin, aren't you," he said, suddenly, the idea having just dawned on him. Her ferocious stare at the blue flower trim on the edge of the quilt must have confirmed his suspicion. "A 27-year-old virgin! Fucking unbelievable!" Michael's voice had lost all its irritation. She had probably been beet-red with embarrassment by that moment.

"Look," he said, and stroked her leg gently. She flinched. "We can do it soft, and slow, whatever you'd like. There's no need to be embarrassed."

"I don't think so," she said tensely.

He continued to stroke her leg. "C'mon, Elizabeth. Why did you invite me over? Don't you ever just want make love?"

She pulled away from him, but he grabbed her arm. She glared at him, angry and more than a little frightened. He no longer had a hold of her arm, but she was frozen; she could not move. There was a moment of hesitation—she felt it from him—and then Michael unbuttoned her blouse, pulled it off, and removed the loose bra. She covered her breasts with her arms. He pushed her back on the bed, gently but deliberately. "You know," he said in a matter-of-fact tone, "I've just had one too many of the yes-no routines. Don't worry. I won't hurt you. I won't *deflower* you." He smirked.

The rest of it… Elizabeth rarely let herself think of it. He had ejaculated on her stomach. It was frightening and repulsive. When he was done he pulled up his jeans, rebuttoned his shirt and left, without another word.

Elizabeth had jumped up and rushed into the shower. Afterward she put on clean clothes and turned on the television just to get sound in the room.

He hadn't raped her, though he could have, she thought.

He hadn't been who she'd thought he was. Luckily, there were only a couple of weeks left in the project and she was able to avoid him. It had been a bad experience, and not one she would expose herself to again, ever.

Chapter 8

Aunt May's Place

Elizabeth finally decided to spend most of her remaining five weeks' vacation fixing up Aunt May's three-family building in Bridgewater. She and her mother spent every weekend and many weeknights at the place on Jasper Street. It took two full weeks to move the furniture into storage. Between the two of them, they de-greased three kitchens, de-mildewed three bathrooms, patched the walls, primed and painted 14 rooms and 20 windows in Linen White, and had the floors on the bottom two flats sanded. Luckily, the outside had been painted only a couple of years ago and was in good repair.

Elizabeth retained memories of Aunt May, but she did not miss her. May had come over from Russia first and had sent for her younger sister Katya the following year. Ten years younger than May, Katya was outgoing and soon learned English, and married Elizabeth's father, an American, within two years. Her father had died when Elizabeth was two, and Aunt May had filled in like a domineering second mother—a father, except for her gender—advising her sister on every aspect of American daily life, from child-raising to savings accounts to unplugging a clogged toilet. As a child, Elizabeth had always been frightened of May; as an adult, she had come to agree with most of her aunt's opinions. Sometimes, lately, Elizabeth felt that her mother had begun to look to her for advice and assurance in the same way as she had her sister.

"Elizabeth, cut your hair!" Aunt May had exclaimed the last time she and her mother visited her in the nursing home, four months ago. "You're a professional woman, and you're almost 50. A woman of that age should not have hair down her back." If it had been anyone else, Elizabeth would have told them to kindly mind their own business. She patted Aunt May's hand.

"Did you know, she had changed her name from Olga when she came over?" her mother had asked one evening when they were working at Aunt May's place. She was down on her knees, scraping layers of paint off the floorboards. At 76, her mother was still amazingly strong. (Sometimes Elizabeth was grateful for this; sometimes it was annoying. A couple of times she had bowed out of administrative gatherings, claiming this sickness or that of her mother's, and then someone from the college had had to reach her. "You must have the wrong Mrs. Wright. *I'm* not sick," Katya Wright would say gruffly to the caller, having picked up on the first ring despite Elizabeth's instructions, and hand over the phone, leaving Elizabeth to fend for herself.)

"No, mother, I didn't know that." She rinsed out her paint brush. It was early spring, and already dark with a forecast of more snow. In the darkened window over the sink, she saw her reflection, her hair in a bun and covered with a scarf. If she wore wire frame glasses instead of contacts she could almost *be* her aunt's reflection. Aunt May had been 37 when Elizabeth was born, more than ten years younger than she was now. She couldn't picture May as an Olga, and now, suddenly tired, she didn't try.

"Yes, she changed her name. Are you *sure* you didn't know that? She changed her name to 'May' because that was the month she arrived here. And it sounded much better to her than 'Olga.'"

"Don't scrape the bare wood down, Mother."

"I'm not." Her mother sighed and sat back on her heels.

Elizabeth wanted to quit for the night, but she wasn't going to stop before her mother.

"I myself thought Olga was a fine name," her mother said. She sighed again. "I think I'm ready to go home and have some dinner."

"That's a good idea," Elizabeth said, holding out her arm to help her mother up.

Her mother hesitated, then took the arm. "I put some beef and vegetables into the crock pot."

"That's good." Elizabeth put on her coat to go warm up the car.

"It's not that cold; we don't need to warm up the car," her mother said. "I'm coming with you." Elizabeth laid out her brushes to dry, and they turned off the lights. She paused for a moment in the dark room as her mother thumped down the stairs. The place was so big, so old and empty. This flat, despite the stairs, had been May's until she moved into the nursing home. Elizabeth remembered getting in trouble tumbling on the oriental carpet as a child. Why had Aunt May been so mean? In her twenties, Elizabeth had thought it might be because May never had children; but Elizabeth's mother, 10 years younger, had two children and she was just as gruff. Perhaps it was something in the genes, the Russian temperament. Hardships.

"I thought you'd slipped, or something," her mother said, waiting outside the car when she got down. Elizabeth couldn't have been more than a couple of minutes. It was completely dark now. She beeped the locks on the Acura and locked the doors again when they were both inside the car. The neighborhood was not so good after dark. Each time she came to work on the house there was another piece of garbage or a broken bottle in the yard. It was only a matter of time before someone broke in. She wanted to sell it as soon as possible.

They drove home to Milport in silence and ate their stew in silence. Elizabeth read the paper while they ate dinner, as she often did. Afterward, Mrs. Wright washed the dishes and Elizabeth watched television. During the months that they were working on Aunt May's place, she often fell asleep in front of the television and her mother would jostle her on her way up to bed.

"You've got work in the morning," she'd say.

Even on the weekends, Mrs. Wright had a tendency to knock lightly on Elizabeth's door and say something like, "We going to breakfast this morning, or not?", and Elizabeth would get up and take a shower and put on slacks instead of a dress or suit, and the two of them would drive down to the diner by the waterfront and have bacon and eggs at a good price. Then, after lunch, they would change into old clothes and head to Bridgewater to work on Aunt May's place. Sundays, Mrs. Wright usually let Elizabeth sleep in.

Finally, the work was done. After a trip to the dump, Elizabeth had spent the morning cleaning out the cellar, leaving a few basic tools such as a broom and mop, the ancient, manual-push lawn mower, and a box of garbage bags. She spent half an hour going through all the rooms, locking and unlocking each apartment, flushing each toilet and surveying her work. Elizabeth enjoyed the feeling of accomplishment at the end.

It was similar to the way she felt when a large federal grant was finally complete—all the narratives finally coming together, the budget, the appendices with their extra demonstrations of project need and potential success. Back in the day it would be all printed, proofed, copied, clipped, packaged and strapped with tape—much more satisfying than the password-accessed online submissions). Elizabeth liked that moment of Fed-Exing the grant almost better than hearing that it had actually been awarded. Usually, an award meant going back into the bowels of the budget and reconfiguring something, and that wasn't her favorite task. She preferred finishing to revising. She knew there were some grant-writers that preferred revising; coming up with new ideas to make the same amount of money work; she had met them at fundraising conferences. But that untidiness wasn't for her. She knew herself; no one would argue that. *You are who you are,* she said sometimes, as her mother had often said to her.

Elizabeth took off her shoes and stepped onto the freshly stained hardwood floor, smooth and gleaming and practically golden in the spring sun. She thought of sliding across the room in her socks, like a child, but she didn't.

Chapter 9

Redecorating

Shortly after she was hired at the college, Elizabeth had five bookcases built for the many Foundation Directories, grant manuals, and publications she received. The varnished pine bookcases weren't at all fancy, but they were very sturdy. She'd hired one of the maintenance men to do the job on the side for a very reasonable price. When her office was moved up to the Admissions Building, though, the room was much smaller and to fit the bookcases she'd had to make a little tunnel of them on one side of the room, the shelves facing each other. Even though it was a tight fit, she liked the way it felt like a little library on that side of the room. She'd even affixed a lamp to one of the shelves for better lighting.

What she hadn't realized was that the back of the bookcases still had the crayon markings of the lumberyard. *72 x 36* was scribbled on each back in blue. And, toward the floor of one of the cases, *Beater.* She did not know what "Beater" signified, and she did not want to know. The crayon scrawl looked vaguely obscene. She'd tried scrubbing them out, and had considered painting them out, but what color? How many coats would it take? All she knew was that she was tired of looking at the markings day after day. Something had to be done. She could feel a project coming over her, a single-mindedness that wouldn't end until the bookcases were covered.

"What do you think about wallpaper on the backs of these bookcases?" she asked Liz one afternoon.

"What do you mean?"

"I mean, I'm thinking of papering the backs of these bookcases. I'm sick of looking at the markings."

"The markings?"

She couldn't believe that Liz hadn't noticed. "There. And there. And look here. There's some kind of lumberyard brand or something near the bottom. I want to cover it over and give us something attractive to look at."

Liz looked doubtful. Obviously she wasn't as interested in decorating as Elizabeth was, although she'd seemed interested when Elizabeth described to her the redecorating of the upstairs of her home. Just last fall she and her mother had stripped the hallway wallpaper themselves and selected a very finely embossed paper in a pale rose color—very expensive, high quality. Elizabeth painted her bedroom herself and found a perfect floral fabric to redo the bed ruffle and canopy. She'd described each room in great detail to Liz, who had watched her, fascinated, occasionally offering up a question about one detail or another.

"Well," Liz said finally, "I've never wallpapered. How would you hold it up?"

"Wallpaper glue would be too messy," Elizabeth realized aloud. "And I don't know that it would hold. Staples, probably."

Liz made a thoughtful noise.

"What *kind* of wallpaper?" she asked.

"I'm not sure. I thought I'd go by the shop and pick up some samples."

41

On her way home from work Elizabeth borrowed the paper book from Mac, who knew her well from her trips to his shop last fall. He was pricey, but she'd know what she was getting. And just to cover bases, she stopped at Home Depot for some cheaper samples. After dinner she pored over the papers, trying to picture each design in the small concrete room. There was a bookcase facade that she was fond of, and a couple of patterns tending toward Victoriana. She'd ask Liz what she thought. She had a moment of doubt when she thought that perhaps Liz wouldn't like the same patterns she'd like, but she decided to present it in such as way as "Here are the three possibilities." It was her office, after all.

Still, she felt uncomfortable showing Liz just the three samples and instead gave her the whole book, with her three choices marked. She wanted Liz to like what she liked.

Liz looked through the book for only a few minutes. "The paper that looks like books would be a little ridiculous," she said. Finally she pointed to Elizabeth's last choice. "This one is okay." It was the vaguely Victoriana sample on the forest green background. Liz shrugged. "It's hard to picture it on the back of the bookcase."

Elizabeth was a little disappointed at Liz's lack of enthusiasm.

"Okay, the green it is," she said.

Elizabeth purchased the wallpaper, but hanging it proved much more difficult than she'd imagined. For two afternoons, instead of working on the database, Liz held the wallpaper in place while Elizabeth stapled it to the backs of the bookcases. When two cases were done, Elizabeth discovered that the paper wasn't exactly straight. She knew if she left it that way it would only bother her until she did something about it, so she took the paper down and started again.

"Are you okay?" she asked Liz, who looked blanched.

"Just a little queasy."

"We can take a break. Why don't you go get a soda?"

Elizabeth looked at her watch. She felt a twinge of guilt about using Liz's work time, but they were into this project now and it was best to go forward. How Liz's time was used didn't make any difference to anyone other than herself, anyway, she thought.

After about fifteen minutes, Liz began to look herself again and they started hanging the paper. Now that she had the rhythm of it, Elizabeth began to enjoy it. They finished two cases the first afternoon, cutting and trimming to fit. She would have stayed late to finish, but she needed Liz to hold the paper for her and she didn't want to ask her to stay.

She even had trouble concentrating on a proposal the next morning, waiting for Liz to come in so they could finish the cases. Even though the wallpaper was dark, it was an improvement to the office. It looked more...regal now, she thought, more official.

She said this to Liz when she came in and Liz shrugged. "I'm not good at this redecorating stuff," she said.

The afternoon passed quickly. Slivers of green paper piled up on the table "like a pile of seaweed," Liz said. Finally, the bookcases were done. The room felt different. Darker, but cleaner.

"It's more professional, don't you think?" she asked Liz.

"Something like that," Liz said, considering.

Chapter 10

Dinner at Liz's

Elizabeth had declined two invitations to come over to Liz's house for dinner. On the third request she accepted. The MacKenzie's lived in the north end of town, in a modest cape. The yard was tidy, except for a couple of those bright plastic riding toys for children and two cars in the short driveway, one without its wheels and the other looked like it wouldn't run. Elizabeth recognized Liz's car in front of the house and parked behind it. Liz came out to meet her.

"You found it!" she exclaimed happily. She was wearing shorts and an oversize T-shirt, from which one could just barely see she was pregnant. A small boy peered out the screen door behind her. "C'mon out, Tyler. This is Elizabeth, who I work with." Tyler continued to examine Elizabeth from behind the screen, and Liz shrugged.

"Elizabeth, don't you have any jeans?" She was frowning in a friendly way at Elizabeth's loose navy-blue slacks and a sailor-type top, with black flats. Actually, she had had a hard time deciding what to wear, and finally settled for this ensemble, which is what she usually wore to casual college functions.

"I don't wear jeans."

"You don't wear jeans? You don't have *any?*"

"Well," she considered, "I have some paint-spattered ones with holes in them for working on my aunt's place, but that's about it. I find them uncomfortable and, for most people, unflattering."

"Well, I'm sure they're unflattering on me!" Liz laughed. "You didn't ever wear jeans, not even in college?"

"Oh, yes, I wore them in graduate school." Elizabeth paused, thinking of that time. When was it? 1967? 1968? "I had this one pair, when I was working at the lab in Johnson Park—holes in the knees, acid burns down the side..."

"A lab in the park?"

"It was a little trailer, actually, set up on the edge of the park. We were analyzing cultures from the pond." They were still standing on the stoop, and Elizabeth was beginning to feel awkward with Tyler staring out at her.

"No kidding," Liz said. She was looking at Elizabeth in a funny way.

"What?"

"Oh, nothing. I was just thinking there's this other you beneath the you."

Elizabeth blushed, remembering Michael Dalaian had said something similar to her. She laughed uneasily.

They heard another door slam in the back of the house and Liz's husband came in. "Well, Tyler, why'nt you tell me the company was here?" Jack opened the screen door and reached out with a warm handshake. "Jack MacKenzie," he said, formally, as though she were a customer.

"Hello, Jack," she said. He was handsome and rough looking, with broad shoulders and dark brown hair flecked with gray. He was very tan. "Elizabeth's been wanting to have you over for a long time," he said.

"Well, it's nice to be here," she replied.

46

It was Jack who escorted Elizabeth around the house. He seemed eager to show her the work he'd done on this "fixer-upper" that he and Liz had purchased two years ago. Probably Liz had told him about the work she was doing on her aunt's place. Liz followed them quietly.

"This room's not very big, but we figure it'll do for the baby," Jack said of a tiny room upstairs with a small window. The previous owners had probably used it as a closet, but Jack and Liz had sanded the floor and painted the walls and the slanted ceiling white with a light blue trim, and the window gave it some light. It was charming, actually.

"A crib and a changing table—that's about it," Liz said. Jack put his big arm around her shoulders and kissed the top of her head.

There were two other bedrooms, plainly disposed and recently cleaned.

Downstairs, Jack poured Elizabeth a glass of white wine, presented it to her with almost a little bow and went out with the marinated steak to "start up the grill."

"He never asks anyone if they want something; he just pours," Liz said, matter-of-fact.

"Well, this is fine," Elizabeth said. She liked Jack, and she liked this modest house. From the chair in the kitchen she could see out the back door. The backyard was twice as big as the front. There was an old swing set in one corner, where Tyler was now twisting himself on the swing. He looked more like his father than he looked like Liz.

There was no dining room, so they ate in the kitchen with a fan on. "I've got to fix that picnic table," Jack apologized. Elizabeth was surprised that the dinner was so delicious. Tyler finally loosened up and told them all a story of how another kid's bicycle had been stolen down the block, and then Jack told the story of how Tyler fell out of a tree and hit his jaw on the fence, and when he saw Elizabeth's horror, Tyler jumped up from the dinner table to find photos of himself smiling with a jaw swollen to twice its size. At that point Liz shooed them all out of the kitchen so that she could clean up and make coffee. She declined Elizabeth's offer to help, and Jack poured Elizabeth another glass of wine, again without asking, but she didn't mind.

She and Jack sat in the darkening living room. It must have been after eight o'clock. "You don't mind if I leave the lights off?" he asked. "It's hot with them on." He turned on another small fan on the floor by the couch. It was actually quite comfortable in the dimness. Elizabeth hadn't had two glasses of wine on the same night in a long time and she felt relaxed and strangely safe in the small room with its old couch, club chair, and the rocker where she sat now. A blue cotton throw on the chair was a cheery touch. Tyler sat cross-legged in the tiny sun porch watching television, and every few moments through the half-open door Elizabeth heard him chuckle. From the kitchen came the sound of water and clinking as Liz washed the dishes.

Jack made conversation, sitting on the couch, at ease. First he talked about his work as a mechanic (he did construction part-time, too, when it was a good job), and Elizabeth asked him questions about where the garage was located, etcetera. Then he asked her how long she'd been teaching—no, working—at the college and did she like her work and did she like her Acura—what was the gas mileage on it?—and had she ever been married.

"No, never married." Apparently Liz had not told him much about her. In one way she was grateful. On the other hand, she did not want to explain how and why she lived with her mother, just now, to Jack.

He didn't ask and instead seemed to contemplate the fact of her being single.

Liz came in with a tray of coffee and fruit with whipped cream and flipped on a lamp. "Jack, we can't see what we're eating," Liz protested. The dessert was fresh and delicious; Elizabeth found herself wanting more, making a note to get some fruit this weekend. The coffee was stronger than she liked it, but they assured her it was decaf.

Liz sat by Jack on the couch, and he put his arm around her fondly. A couple of times he patted Liz on the stomach when she referred to January, when the baby was due. Liz felt certain it was another boy and they might name it Luke. "Jack doesn't like the name Luke," Liz said, briefly capturing his hand. Elizabeth was beginning to feel uncomfortable with these displays of affection. As if she sensed it, Liz moved to the other end of the couch.

Another half hour passed peacefully and it was 10 o'clock. Liz was yawning and she looked suddenly very tired. Surprised at the late hour, Elizabeth stood up and said her farewells. As she started her car, they waved to her, framed in the light of the front porch, and she waved back and heard Jack say something to Liz and then the words *elegant woman*. Somehow, over the noise of the engine through the night air, the words came to Elizabeth as if directed to her. She felt

49

strange and pleased the way she had earlier in the evening, and drove all the way home feeling this way.

Chapter 11

The Phans

Such a routine of working at Aunt May's place had been established that Elizabeth felt slightly at a loss talking to the real estate agent, Marlene Parisi. "Don't spend any more time on this place, Ms. Wright," she said, accenting the "Miz". "It looks great, but I can't hold out a lot of hope for a quick sell. Nothing's like it used to be in Bridgewater."

At first Elizabeth ignored the comment as typical real estate advice. But after four months and no offers whatsoever, they lowered the price. After another two months, Marlene advised them to go even lower. When there were no bids after that, Marlene asked them if they had thought about renting out the three apartments, and after many phone calls she convinced Elizabeth and her mother to rent. The market was down, and the neighborhood was deteriorating. "But I won't go below $800 a month for the lower flats, and $500 for the studio," Elizabeth said.

"That might be hard," Marlene countered.

And indeed, after two months and no suitable renters (Marlene was screening applicants), Elizabeth was almost ready to accept anything. Each week she stopped by the building and checked the locks, swept the front porch and cleaned up garbage to give the place a lived-in look. She had a timed porch light installed and had even considered putting up curtains, but stopped herself. The porch light had been broken twice by thrown rocks. Elizabeth hated to think of the gleaming floors and fresh white walls gathering dust.

Marlene called one day in the middle of October. "I have a proposition for you," she said. "Hear me out." Under a new subsidy for immigrants, a City agency would guarantee half the rent for one year for qualified immigrants in apartments renting for $700 or less. Marlene had had a Vietnamese family referred to her, and she thought immediately of Elizabeth's place.

"Let me think about it," Elizabeth said.

That evening, her mother shrugged and went back to her dishes. "It's not what I would have wanted," she said.

Elizabeth even asked Liz what she thought. Liz spoke Spanish and was generally more liberal in racial matters. "It sounds interesting," Liz had said. "Besides, you don't have a whole lot of choice, do you? Except to leave it vacant?"

The next day, Elizabeth found out more about the proposed family. Phan Tuan was in his 30's, with a wife, three children, and his mother-in-law. They had been in the U.S. for four months and the City of Bridgewater was helping Mr. Phan look for work. In Vietnam, he had been a certified engineer. Marlene had met him and portrayed him as a decent person who would respect property. Elizabeth didn't know how six people could fit in a flat designed for three, or perhaps four, but she decided not to worry about that at present. She had Marlene arrange a meeting at Aunt May's place.

Elizabeth arrived after work before the others and went through the building, unlocking doors and opening the windows to let some air in, even though it was chilly. They were late; that didn't bode well, she thought. After she had been there about fifteen minutes, Marlene's car pulled up to the curb and Phan Tuan and his entire family disembarked. Marlene gave her an apologetic look from the curb. Introductions were made on the porch.

"A pleasure, Miss Wright." Mr. Phan wore thick black glasses and spoke limited English. He was very short, around 5.3, and Elizabeth had the urge to remove her heels to feel less imperious. His wife, whose name she didn't catch, was even shorter and stood partially behind her husband, bowing slightly every time Elizabeth looked in her direction. Mr. Phan pointed to Marlene's car, where just above the window Elizabeth could make out a red knit cap and a worried face. "My mother remains in car. No chair in apartment Miss Wright show."

The two older children had none of this obsequiousness and did not even come up to the porch for introductions, running instead up and down the grassy alleyway to the backyard like animals that had been in cramped quarters. The youngest girl, however, remained quietly beside her father on the porch. Elizabeth found herself looking frequently at the child. She made a point of smiling, and eventually the little girl smiled hesitantly back at her. Mr. Phan noticed her attentions and pushed the child forward. "This Lucy," he said. "She good girl, not like those crazies," he added, referring, Elizabeth supposed, to the other two children. Lucy had huge brown eyes and perfect olive skin and was wearing a short-sleeved blue dress that was too big for her and too lightweight for the chilly air. She nodded at Elizabeth, then stepped back close to her father. Elizabeth imagined a sweater for her—a cozy, white cotton sweater.

"Let's go in, then," she said. The mother came alive at that point, yelling harshly in Vietnamese to the children, who joined them in a hurry. Elizabeth showed them quickly through the two lower flats, knowing that the top was too small. Mr. Phan asked to see it anyway, chattering busily in Vietnamese to his wife as they went. He seemed to be explaining much more than the simple comments that Elizabeth and Marlene were giving. To Elizabeth's relief, his wife demanded that the children take off their shoes on the hardwood floors, and they slid across the room the way Elizabeth had imagined doing last year when she'd finished fixing up the place. Even shy Lucy tried a slide or two. Elizabeth enjoyed the children's pleasure and felt suddenly more kindly toward Mr. Phan and his wife. Then she remembered the mother in the car. "Your mother!" she exclaimed.

Mr. Phan put up his hand in dismissal. "She probably sleep. It is okay."

It was agreed. They made arrangements for a move-in date the following week. Marlene was going to assist them. As part of the arrangement with the City, there would be no security deposit; since they were moving in on the second of the month, rent would be due on the second day of each month. Marlene stressed that there would be no additional people living in the flat, and Mr. Phan nodded happily to each agreement as he signed the papers.

Elizabeth spent a whole hour the next morning telling Liz about the meeting with the Phan's. Liz patted her pregnant belly thoughtfully. "Well, they sound interesting. And the most you could lose would be $350 a month."

"You think they won't pay?" Elizabeth was alarmed to think Liz would be thinking that way, although the thought had crossed her mind, too.

"Oh, I don't know. It'll probably be fine. Interesting, at least." Elizabeth didn't like the way Liz kept using the word *interesting* these days.

Chapter 12

The Phans' Bathtub

Elizabeth waited one extra day after the Phans moved in before arriving to check on them and pick up the first month's rent. Marlene had called to say the move had been easy; they had hardly any furniture. This certainly turned out to be the case. One of the children, the boy, answered her knock and opened the door a crack, eyeing her suspiciously.

"Hello, I don't remember your name. It's Miss Wright," Elizabeth said, rather more loudly than she needed to. "Tell your father it's Miss Wright at the door."

The boy ran upstairs and there was a brief racket before Mr. Phan came down in his socks which she noted were red and covered with tiny Santa Clauses. "Oh, Miss Wright," he said, beaming. "Come in." He led her up the stairs to her Aunt May's old apartment, having chosen it over the lower one which Elizabeth had thought would have been easier for his elderly mother-in-law.

There were seven pairs of shoes lined up by the door. Elizabeth removed her pumps and put them in the line, hoping to please them. Mrs. Phan smiled at her and nodded vigorously. Not knowing what to do with her pocketbook, she kept it on her shoulder.

"Hello," Elizabeth said, extending her hand. "It's nice to see you again." Mr. Phan translated, and his wife nodded again.

Elizabeth had never felt so large in her aunt's place. A straw mat was laid in the center of the room, which was sadly furnished with one lime-green, thread-bare couch and two twin-size mattresses covered with multicolored sheets, head-to-head against the windowed wall. Another sheet hung in the hallway leading to the two back bedrooms. Elizabeth would have liked to see how they had arranged her Aunt's rooms, but she remembered it was not technically "her" place anymore.

"This is my mother," Mr. Phan said, introducing the tiny woman who sat on the couch, her small feet in white socks dangling about six inches from the ground. She wore the same red knit cap as she had in Marlene's car.

"How do you do?" Elizabeth gave a nod in the woman's direction.

The woman looked at her, then looked out the window.

"My mother is sad," Mr. Phan said, simply. He didn't seem to feel any additional information was necessary, and then Lucy appeared from behind the sheet, rubbing her eyes. "Ah, Lucy," Mr. Phan said, putting his hands on her shoulders. "She take a lot naps here. I look for work," he interrupted himself suddenly, as though Elizabeth had asked him a question. He pointed emphatically to the newspaper on the arm of the couch. She hadn't thought of the fact that they might not have a computer. Hopefully the agency was helping them out in looking for work.

"Oh," he interrupted himself again. "We have difficulty bath. You fix for us?" He beckoned Elizabeth to follow him behind the sheet.

The hallway was dark, with boxes piled up in front of both bedroom doors. Mr. Phan took her into the bathroom. It wasn't the bath that had a problem; it was the toilet which was running. Elizabeth showed Mr. Phan how to jiggle the handle and opened the top of the toilet to show him the mechanism.

"Oh!" he exclaimed. "Very simple."

Elizabeth noted what seemed to be a gray film on the bathtub and bent over to examine it. It wasn't dirt, as she feared, but scratches. "What are you using to clean this tub?" Elizabeth asked, rather sharply. Scratches could not be removed.

Mr. Phan, flustered, yelled loudly in Vietnamese for his wife, who came running. He translated Elizabeth's question. Mrs. Phan ran back to the kitchen and held up a scouring pad, chattering quickly and bowing toward Elizabeth. Mr. Phan translated that his son had gotten very dirty, had taken a bath, and that his wife had tried to clean the film left in the tub.

"Oh, but you can't use a pad like this. See how it scratches!"

Mrs. Phan wrung her hands and nodded gravely.

"Well, never mind," Elizabeth said, standing up, tugging awkwardly on her pocketbook still slung on her shoulder. She brushed her hands lightly on her suit skirt. "Next time I come I will bring something proper to clean with. Don't use this anymore."

Mr. Phan assured her they wouldn't. "I also have money," he said. "For you." Elizabeth was greatly relieved she wasn't going to have to ask directly for the first month's rent. As she put on her pumps, he went into one of the bedrooms and came out with a stack of cash: tens, twenties, and ones. Elizabeth folded the money discreetly and put it in her pocketbook.

Four blocks from the house, she couldn't stand it anymore. She pulled the car over to the side of the road, put on her emergency blinkers, and counted the money. $350. It was all there. Elizabeth let out a sigh of relief. That, at least, was a good start.

Chapter 13

The Office Must Move

Elizabeth did not like Jim Lindell's eyes, and that was just the beginning of what she did not like. They were gray and milky and would never settle for more than a second on anything. Especially when he was talking to someone (in this case, her), they would start with the face, then flick over to the shoulder, to some spot behind the head, then back to the mouth and then finally an eye-to-eye, at which point he would usually smile as he made his point. But the smile never rose to his eyes. They were sealed gray orbs. Elizabeth imagined him popping them out and polishing them in his office.

Lindell had been Vice President of Advancement for one year. The VP before him, Larry Simpson, had had similar eyes and more ambition. Two years in a small college had been enough for him. Lindell, on the other hand, appeared to be at the college for the long haul. He was slim, stylishly gray, and exercised a boyish appeal in groups. Older women and alumni, the primary donors to the school, loved him. He was appropriately, generically religious (Episcopalian), married to a blonde woman named Pam, and had four daughters.

Liz had gone down to the main administration building on some errands and so Elizabeth was alone when Lindell made his unexpected visit. He seated himself in the leather chair that was wedged between the two desks. She offered him some tea, which he declined. To keep busy in front of him,

Elizabeth made herself some, pouring hot water over a Lipton's bag in a paper cup, adding a dab of evaporated milk and a spoon full of sugar. She then sat down slowly behind her desk.

"So, what brings you to our neck of the woods, Jim?" she said pleasantly.

"How's that new girl—Liz—working out?" he asked, absentmindedly, ignoring her question. Liz had only been at the college for *nine* months, she thought, irritated.

"I'm very pleased."

"Well, we like to have you pleased, Elizabeth."

Lindell was examining the wallpaper covering the bookcases, so he didn't see the frozen gaze she directed his way, although she was certain he knew she was looking at him.

"As you know, they're building us a very spacious office over at the main building," Lindell said. "And I'd like you and your assistant to move down with us." Now he turned to her and Elizabeth found herself looking at an old burned-in coffee ring on her institution-issue desk.

"Frankly," he continued (he was never frank in his whole life, she thought), "I really feel you're too isolated here; I'd like to have your input and feedback on other projects in the Development area. You bring in a lot of money for the school, Elizabeth, and I, for one, really appreciate how hardworking you are. We could use more people like you on board, and I'm working toward that end. I don't know if I told you, I'm interviewing for a new Annual Giving person and someone to do research, and we have some good candidates lined up. That's what *I've* been doing lately...."

Elizabeth could feel Lindell losing his point, and she shifted her stare back to him.

"So," Lindell stood up suddenly, as if they had had a long, definitive conversation, "we are all moving in January, after the holidays. There's a suite that will do nicely for you and your assistant—you'll have your own office!— and I encourage you to come down and take a look at the area and begin making your floorplans.

"Oh, and I was wondering. Your monthly reports? Could you do them in a larger type size? They're damn hard to read." He stood there a moment, awaiting a response.

Was he really telling her this? Did he ever *read* her reports? "Yes, I can do that," Elizabeth said, finally.

"I'll just let myself out," Lindell said cheerfully, as though it were a long way out and the room wasn't crowded with bulky desks and bookcases.

His hand was on the knob. "Jim," she said abruptly. "Do I have any say in this move at all?"

Lindell paused, frowned, and rubbed the back of his head with his hand—another of his boyish gestures. "Frankly, no. The orders come from *my* boss." He shrugged.

"Tom?" She stood up.

Lindell smiled sadly in affirmation and left before she could ask or say more, closing the door quietly behind him.

So why couldn't he say "Tom"? She'd known Tom McNamara longer than he had. She'd known the two presidents before him, too. Tom McNamara had been the president for the past three years and was on an image-building campaign for the college that baffled Elizabeth and excited alumni. Why he would want to turn a community school that successfully served older and remedial students into the next booming liberal arts mecca was beyond her. Or, rather, it wasn't. Money. And local prestige that might grow past local. There were rumors about Tom running for some political office after he turned the school around. She had to admit a twinge of pleasure herself when another news article about the college and its expansions appeared in the local paper. She had been called and quoted a couple of times—on the Upward Bound program and the high school science teachers program. In her 20 years there, she had been instrumental—a grant word, but accurate—in getting those two major programs underway.

And now they were moving her. Without the decency to consult her.

Elizabeth sat back down, rigid. She had been holding on to the paper cup, squeezing it, and now tea was leaking out the bottom. She found a paper towel to clean it up and by the time she was finished, Liz came back from her errands. Her face was flushed from the cold air, and with her bulky coat it was difficult to tell that she was seven months along.

"I saw Lindell coming down the walk," she said, breathless.

"Yes."

"He kind of smiled at me, but I don't think he had a clue who I was." She hung up her coat.

"I'm sure that's so."

"What's wrong?"

Elizabeth gave a small disgusted snort. "He informed me that the Grants Office is moving down with the rest of Advancement into the new space they're building down there."

"What?"

"And, furthermore, he doesn't understand our reports."

"Why does he want to move you?"

"*Us.*"

"Us," Liz repeated, blankly.

"Oh, he mumbled something about more input, blah blah blah." Still standing, Elizabeth fussed about her desk, aligning her notepads, retrieving stray paperclips and putting them into the container.

"I am," she paused, "extremely irritated."

"I can see that," Liz said simply, remaining standing. "Maybe we should just go down to the space and see what it's about," she said, after a moment. "There has to be an awful lot of room to hold those file cabinets."

This was true; it was likely that Lindell hadn't thought of the little room full of file drawers. However, right now she didn't want to give him the time of day. And she didn't want word to get to him that Elizabeth was examining the space, because that would mean she'd capitulated. At least she no longer felt like she wanted to throw something.

"I don't think so," she said, sounding more abrupt than she meant to. "Not today. I have too much to do."

Liz shrugged and settled in to finish the grants newsletter. Elizabeth did not have pressing work, and she knew she wouldn't be able to concentrate. Nevertheless, she managed to tidy up the outline for Sahil's latest proposal and so she and Liz spent the last hour of the day each at their own machine, the only sounds being the clicking of keyboards and occasional squeak of an office chair.

Chapter 14

That's All There Is to It

On Thanksgiving morning, her brother Thomas had driven up from Philadelphia and they all went to dinner at the same restaurant where they had gone with Aunt May the past few years. Last year, Thomas had been on-call and had been unable to come, and May had been too sick to go out. Elizabeth and her mother had brought her leftovers from the restaurant.

Thomas was a neurosurgeon, and he was always busy. He had never married. Elizabeth had occasionally wondered about that, but over time she realized she didn't want to know more. They were not close. She recognized herself in him in the way his eyes were close together, but his hair was black, like their father's had been. Thomas was tall and skinny and always looked distracted, like he wanted to be somewhere else.

Still, Elizabeth was glad to have Thomas there at dinner, which had been mostly just fine; they had even shared a bottle of wine. Mrs. Wright was surprised, again, at the number of people who went out for the holiday meal. "Must cost them ten times what it would cost to cook," she said, shaking her head, as if the main cause for eating out were laziness. Thomas retorted, rather more sharply than necessary, that many people would prefer to spend the time together talking, rather than jumping up every five seconds to fill up a plate or adjust the oven temperature, and Mrs. Wright was quiet.

In the silence that followed Elizabeth recalled how her mother had always said to her and Thomas, "When *I* was growing up we learned how to work hard." It was their mother's song, her litany; she and Thomas were used to it. The unsaid statement, of course, being that they were both lazy children. Nothing made Mrs. Wright more angry than laziness, and she wasn't above a quick smack on their rears with a rolled newspaper when Thomas defied her, which was often. It was usually over some chore he hadn't done, or being late. Elizabeth remembered watching her mother remove sections of the paper so she could handle the roll more adeptly.

Elizabeth had avoided the roll, but not the hand. Once— she had been about 7 or 8—she had left a pile of clothes on the floor in her room. That would have been bad enough, except for the damp towel on the bottom of the pile, which left a huge black spot on the hardwood. She'd been in her room, sitting on her bed, brushing her hair, when her mother came in.

"I've asked a hundred times: bring your clothes down to the basement. You're not a baby. I can't do all the chores around this house." It was the familiar refrain, but this time for some reason her voice had risen high as she said it, her face enlivened into someone Elizabeth had never seen before. She strode across the room, grabbed Elizabeth fiercely by the upper arm, lifting her off the bed and smacked her several times on her back and rear. Elizabeth was so startled that she didn't call out or even cry, and then suddenly her mother had stopped, picked up the pile of clothes, and left the room.

At dinner that night Mrs. Wright had been her normal self. The peas and meatloaf were passed. Weekly chores and school activities for Elizabeth and Thomas were discussed. Nothing out of the ordinary was said. If the four yellow bruises hadn't appeared on Elizabeth's arm the next day, she wouldn't have been sure it ever happened.

Now Thomas broke the silence at their table in the restaurant by describing his new condominium and extending an invitation to them to visit. Mrs. Wright nodded and smiled and said that everything sounded attractive and convenient. Elizabeth hadn't visited Thomas at his place since she was in graduate school. Now, a visit to Pennsylvania meant staying in a motel overnight, which Mrs. Wright would not like. And so, Elizabeth thought dryly, they would not visit, and they would probably not see Thomas again until next Thanksgiving. Every Christmas he went skiing in Colorado. When she or his mother asked about the trip, he was always very vague about details, saying this was the only week he and two colleagues could get the ski cabin.

Elizabeth wondered if he actually went anywhere.

After dinner, they went home for dessert (Mrs. Wright had made a pie), watched a little television, and then Thomas got ready to drive home. He embraced his mother, and Elizabeth put on a jacket and walked out with him. In the driveway, she asked Thomas if his new condo had an extra garage, referring to the sore subject of his pristine 1964 Mustang which took up most of the space in his mother's small garage. He had bought the vintage car when he finished med school. In all the years she had lived with her mother, Elizabeth had never been able to park her car in the garage. Thomas shrugged. "I'll get to it. This spring. I'll get it down there."

"That would be nice."

"How's mother doing, really," Thomas asked, this being the first time they were alone.

It was Elizabeth's turn to shrug. She did not say that he should be around more, because she knew it would make everyone crazy. Besides, the car door was open; Thomas did not want to talk, really.

"Call her now and them. She'd like that," she said, simply. "And thank you for dinner," she added, since Thomas had picked up the tab. She raised her hand in a goodbye and watched Thomas drive down the block, stop briefly at the corner and pull out quickly onto the main road that led to the interstate.

They must be very dull company for him, Elizabeth thought. However, everyone had their obligations. At least he had asked about their mother.

At dinner a few years ago, after a large glass of wine, Elizabeth asked her mother about the childhood incident with the clothes. "Mother, do you remember that time where I'd left a damp towel at the bottom of a pile of clothes, and you were so angry you grabbed me and smacked me?"

Mrs. Wright' gray eyes had widened slightly. She dabbed at her mouth with her napkin. "Why do you bring up something like that?" she asked. It wasn't clear whether she remembered or not. They had finished their dessert together in silence, looking out at the darkening parking lot of the diner. Then her mother had sighed. "It was a long time ago. It's hard bringing up two kids by yourself, and that's all there is to it."

Chapter 15

The Birdbath

The Friday after Thanksgiving was always tedious for Elizabeth. She could tell that Mrs. Wright was disappointed that Thomas didn't stay over. She cleaned the house more than necessary and Elizabeth heard some bumping downstairs and went down to find her mother repapering the cabinet shelves in the kitchen. At that point it was already afternoon and she decided to go out food shopping and stop in at Aunt May's place.

At the store she bought some cleanser and non-scratch pads to deliver to the Phan's. She wondered if they had heeded her warning not to clean the tub with a regular scour pad. She was eager to get there and show them what to do. When she got there, however, around 4 o'clock, no one was home. The big blue car was missing. Elizabeth rang the bell anyway. She could leave the cleanser in a bag with a note, but who knows whether someone would come by and take it, or whether Mr. Phan would really be able to read the note. Really, how did these people survive? she wondered. She then considered letting herself in with her key but decided against it. It *was* her place, but she did not live here, and she herself would be livid if a landlord let himself into a place that *she* was renting...

Still, she was irritated that no one was home. She imagined them seeing her coming and all piling into the blue car and driving off. Elizabeth shook her head. Her thoughts were ridiculous. She let herself into the cellar and looked around. All was as she last left it. She saw the rake and decided to rake up the leaves in the small back yard. She put on some garden gloves she kept in the cellar. She had done a good raking on her last visit and so there was not much to do, but it felt good to move about in the dusky air.

As she made a small pile in one corner of the yard, Elizabeth noticed that the bird bath was missing. It was a white plastic contraption formed to look like marble, about waist-height, weighted in its hollow base with a bag (carefully wrapped in plastic) of concrete mix. The bird bath had been in the middle of the yard last time she was here, and she had been considering whether to store it and had decided to wait. She went back to the cellar and took a closer look around but didn't see it. Elizabeth was irked. She had planned to move that bird bath to her own house for next spring. Obviously, someone had taken it—she imagined two teenagers toppling it, rolling it down the street... and then she felt a wave of irritation that the Phans didn't prevent this from happening. But how would they, Elizabeth asked herself. What did she expect from them? She started raking on the other side, vigorously, and in a few minutes she felt calmer. A new bird bath would not cost that much money, and she'd save the trouble of having to wash the old one.

It was cold, even for November. Snow was forecast for Sunday afternoon. Elizabeth could feel her fingers getting swollen in the thin garden gloves. She had often cleaned and mowed this yard. It was as familiar to her as her own... as her mother's place. Until about six years ago, they had always had Thanksgiving dinner here. It was May's holiday, since

Christmas was spent "with the children" at Mrs. Wright's. From this they understood that Thanksgiving was for adults. May was an excellent cook, and Elizabeth and Thomas would be dutifully awed at the perfect moistness of the turkey, which was big enough for 12 people, and the new stuffing recipe. Their mother would bake the pies. When they were adults, Elizabeth and Thomas would then take a little walk around the block and catch up (this was often the only time they saw each other all year), and come back and watch television for a couple of hours together with their mother and aunt.

Elizabeth didn't miss Aunt May, that much she knew. She missed the gathering, the delicious smells. What would become of them, herself and her mother? She raked up something thick and soggy and held it up gingerly in the darkening sky. It was a child's sock, red. She wondered if it was the girl's—Lucy's. She hadn't seen the child on her last visit, although she'd brought a bag of peppermints just in case.

She turned around and looked up at the apartment and was startled to see the grandmother in the window, looking down at her, the apartment dark behind her. The woman gazed at her for a moment, then withdrew. So someone *was* home. But they had probably told her not to answer the door; that was understandable. How long had the woman been watching her?

Elizabeth looked at the window for another minute, confused by a flickering blue light in the room that she finally realized was a television. The evening had begun to feel distorted, and she couldn't tell what time it was. She placed the red sock on the back porch, carefully. She finished bagging the small pile of leaves and lugged the bag to the trunk of her car. She would leave them at the end of the drive at her house, where there was a better chance the bag would not be kicked in and leaves lost everywhere. It was on her way back that she noticed the cable hanging from the side of the house. Her gaze followed it up to the second floor, where she could see a small hole had been drilled. Mr. Phan, the inexpert engineer, Elizabeth thought, hooking on an extra cable line. This act of subterfuge was both obvious and unattractive. She wondered if she would be liable for charges if the cable company discovered the extra hook-up.

Well, she would have to speak to him, but there was no dealing with it tonight. She left the cleanser on the front porch with a note, *For the bathtub*. She was almost to her car when Elizabeth remembered the sock, retrieved it from the back porch and put it on the front porch with the cleanser.

Chapter 16

Not Too Personal

The time between Thanksgiving and Christmas was usually a strange and empty time for Elizabeth. She knew that many other people experienced a similar emptiness, but she couldn't see them experiencing it. Instead, she felt the excitement of preparation around her. The neighbors who'd lived next door to them for ten years now—otherwise pleasant, quiet people—set up a winter Santa scene on their tiny patch of front yard, with a blinking Rudolf nose that they left on all night until New Year's. At the college, decorations went up for both Christmas and Hanukkah and the Kwaanza holiday (whatever *that* was—another marketing scheme so that everyone would have an excuse to buy things). There would be the two obligatory parties: one at the president's house, and the other down at the Development office—she'd have to attend one, and could feign busyness or illness to get out of the other. The secretaries in the administrative offices down the hill were high-voiced and full of chitchat over this little gift or that and used the holiday to full advantage as an excuse to start work later and stop sooner.

Liz was not like that. In her part-time hours she was quiet, mostly, attentive to her work. She did not go on and on about the baby, but was polite to inquiries about her health, etc., from people who stopped by the office. Elizabeth found herself feeling oddly proud of Liz for being that way, for missing hardly any days during her pregnancy. It was, she realized, the way she herself would behave if she were in Liz's position.

In this affectionate mood Elizabeth had perused the mall on her lunch hour over several days looking for the right Christmas gift for Liz. The gift would have to be modest, in keeping with the amount of time Liz had been working for her, and not too personal—not jewelry or a scarf or bath items—since their relationship was through work. The gift was therefore more difficult to get than Elizabeth expected. There were plenty of kitchen items, but most were out of the modest range. Finally, she settled on a small jam pot and ceramic spoon, and a jar of excellent raspberry jam. After another hour of shopping, she decided to buy one for her mother, too. Since she and her brother did not exchange gifts, that was it for gift shopping. Elizabeth went into a few shops with the intent of purchasing a little something for the Phan's daughter, Lucy, but hesitated after thinking about how it might seem to them—this older woman giving a gift, however simple, to their daughter. Perhaps they would think it an incentive to be late with the rent again (November and December had been late), and Elizabeth decided that it would be inappropriate.

She did find some nice decorations, though: a porcelain Victorian angel with the slightest dust of glitter (which cost more than the jam pot, she noted with a tinge of guilt), a tablecloth (their old Christmas cloth was getting shabby) and holiday napkin rings, some brass candlesticks and potpourri. Both she and her mother liked a festive house, and they usually spent the first Saturday in December decorating the house. Whatever decorations were left over Elizabeth brought to the office. Sometimes Elizabeth could convince her mother to go with her to get a tree, but her mother said she found a tree too much work for just the two of them.

She was now late, and wondered if she should call in to the office. It was one thing she did not like about having an assistant. In those two months where she had no one, she could be late at lunch and no one would notice. Of course, most of the time she didn't even take a lunch, so why would she ever have to justify herself? Elizabeth felt suddenly irritable and sat down on one of the wooden benches outside the coffee place. She could smell the coffee and decided to have a cappuccino—Liz was always buying them, in spite of the expense. Elizabeth had only had one cappuccino before; it had been delicious, and afterward she'd had trouble sleeping. But today there was the whole afternoon and evening ahead... Again she felt irritable.

Two girls walked by, each with a stroller. One carriage held an infant, and the other child was at least two years old. One girl was skinny; the other was enormous. Neither could be over 20, Elizabeth observed. The toddler let out a shriek for some reason, and the skinny girl slapped the child on the head so suddenly that Elizabeth was startled. Her eyes filled with tears. She brushed them away with her napkin. She felt sorry for the child, to grow up with a mother like that. No education, no common sense, *nothing* going for her. *They ought to be sterilized,* her mother would say. The skinny woman looked abruptly over her shoulder at Elizabeth and glared as if she had heard these thoughts.

Elizabeth blushed and swallowed, chastened but still angry, and glad it was a public place. Over the mall speakers, Frank Sinatra sang "Walking in a Winter Wonderland." She heard the jingle of bells at the Santa Center downstairs in the mall. Another afternoon she might have spent a quarter-hour watching the kids, in awe, pose for a photo with Santa. She hoped Liz's baby would be a girl—even though Liz protested it was another boy. In fact, although she had nothing to base her feelings on, Elizabeth felt sure it was a girl. The due date was only six weeks away now. Certainly Liz and Jack would do a good job as parents, as they had already with their boy. She thought of the little room Jack had fixed up for the baby and the modest, clean house.

"You want to feel the baby?" Liz had said last Tuesday.

"Well..."

Liz had grabbed Elizabeth's hand and pressed it to her belly. For a second all she could feel was the warm, slightly moist pressure of Liz's hand. Her belly was surprisingly, amazingly tight, and then she felt a kick and she instinctively pulled away but Liz pressed her hand and she felt another thump, bigger and stranger, extending beyond the reach of her hand.

"He rolled over for you!" Liz smiled brightly, letting go of her hand. Elizabeth would have liked to feel the baby moving again but didn't want to ask.

Elizabeth blinked and realized she had been sitting on the bench for half an hour. That was it, she thought. Her mother had asked her last week what she was going to buy for Liz and the baby. She would get Liz a diaper bag. She almost wanted to shop for it right now, but it really was late and she wanted to be able to take her time. By now, Liz would be at the office, probably wondering where she was, and when she came in Liz would see the bags and ask what she'd purchased, and Elizabeth would show her the decorations (the jam pots safely stashed in the trunk of her car), and they would spend a good hour talking about gift giving.

She would also take Liz out to lunch, she decided, a holiday lunch. That's when she would give her the jam pot. Cheered by these plans, Elizabeth finished her cappuccino, now cold, and headed back to campus.

Chapter 17

The New Space

By the following week, Elizabeth had received two phone calls from Lindell about the new space: had she visited it, what did she think? Each time, Elizabeth returned the call with a message through his secretary that she hadn't had a chance to get down there. On the third call from Lindell's office, Liz asked her, "Don't you think you should check the space out?"

"Actually," Elizabeth said, "I have. And I thought maybe we could go down there together this afternoon and measure it."

Liz looked at her strangely, as if to ask her why she hadn't told Lindell, and Elizabeth shrugged. "I don't like people on my back," she said. "I like to know what I'm getting into before I'm asked to respond."

She had actually gone down there the day after Lindell's visit. She had stayed late and asked Harvey, the head maintenance man, to let her into the building. Apparently, Institutional Advancement was becoming more important to President McNamara, since the new space practically doubled Lindell's current quarters, including Elizabeth's square footage.

She didn't want Liz slipping on any black ice, so Elizabeth drove them the short distance down to the main Administration building. It was after 4:30 and dark; the building was mostly empty. The new offices were at the end of the corridor. The sheetrock was not up in all places, but the wiring was in and luckily there were pieces of paper taped to doorways labeling which office was which. Elizabeth stepped gingerly in her heels across the structuring at the "GRANTS" sign. The office was at least a third bigger than the area she and Liz now shared. Through a connecting door there was another, smaller space with room for a desk and a few file drawers for Liz. Each of their rooms had its own entrance. In Elizabeth's space there were three large windows looking out on a bank of trees and a small corner of the main parking lot.

"I can't believe how big it is!" Liz exclaimed. Elizabeth measured her space while Liz wandered around the overall department, making comments as she went from room to room. "I think yours is the biggest, Elizabeth." She then measured Liz's office to see how many file cabinets would fit in it and still leave room for the desk and computer table. "I think he's trying to make you happy, Elizabeth," Liz called out from Lindell's new office, a rectangle midway in the bank of offices, and half the size of Elizabeth's.

"That might be so," Elizabeth said under her breath.

"Who are all these offices for?" Liz asked, returning to their space. "I didn't know there were that many people in the department."

"Well, I hear he's got plans to hire two new people right away—for research and for annual giving."

"Let's see what it's like in the dark," Liz said, and turned out the lights. They both stood by the dark window in Elizabeth's new office and watched a few stray cars leave the parking lot. Final exams were almost over, and most of the students had left for winter break. It was Elizabeth's favorite time on campus, when everyone was gone.

"So what do you think?" Liz asked.

"What do *you* think?" Elizabeth asked back. In her mind, she was already placing the furniture and felt the familiar tingle of excitement at a new project. She would like to put most of the file drawers into Liz's area, but there probably wasn't enough room. Tomorrow she would get out her graphing paper and do a diagram. She liked doing that. In fact, she admitted to herself, the whole project of moving into this better space would be exciting if it weren't for the proximity of the other development people—Lindell, Cathy DeFranco, the public relations director, and the cadre of new people Lindell was in the process of hiring. She knew she wasn't going to like working near these people, much less *with* them. She was going to have to find a way to be "cooperative" and maintain her distance.

"It's not so bad," Liz answered. "No more long hikes down the hill. Oh, look. There's a back exit right outside this office."

Elizabeth had noted that back door with relief on her first visit. Perhaps they would be able to come and go through this door. In her mind she prepared the email she would send to Lindell, telling him she had examined the space, found it adequate, and was enclosing a list of requirements for the move.

Chapter 18

The Body's Leaks

Liz's water broke three weeks early, just after the Christmas break, as they were packing boxes to move the office. Elizabeth heard the exclamation—a short little "Oh!" in the tunnel of bookshelves—and came around to find Liz standing in a small puddle, her brown leggings stained darker with fluid.

"Well, here we go," Liz said, and giggled slightly. She put her hand over her mouth.

"What can I do?" Elizabeth asked, her heart beating fast.

"There's nothing *to* do, really. I sure wish I had some extra clothes. I have to call Jack. He'll come and get me."

"Do you want me to call him?"

"No, that's okay. I'll call him." Liz waddled slowly toward her desk. She giggled again.

"I'll get some paper towels," Elizabeth said.

"Get a bunch of them, and I'll put some in my pants. This is a mess."

When Elizabeth returned with the paper towels, Liz was on the phone to Jack and seemed more herself.

"He's on his way," she said cheerfully, taking the paper towels from Elizabeth and deftly slipping them into the crotch of her pants. "I don't want to waddle down to the bathroom," Liz explained. "I don't want anyone asking any questions." Curiosity from the employees in the Admissions office had grown since the holidays had passed. Elizabeth saw it as yet another way for mediocre workers to distract themselves from work. She resolved not to tell anyone Liz had gone into labor.

"Are you in pain?" Elizabeth wondered how Liz would look when she was in pain.

"Oh, no. That's for later," she said and smiled. Liz's face was pink and glowing. "Right now it just kind of feels all sucked up, you know? All tight and compressed since that water's gone."

Elizabeth remembered the puddle on the carpet. She couldn't expect Liz to get down there on her hands and knees and clean it up. On the other hand, it seemed rude to clean it up while Liz was still here.

"Twenty-four hours," Liz was saying. "They like to get the baby out within 24 hours after the water breaks—otherwise, there's a risk of infection."

Then Jack arrived in the doorway, his face glowing much the same way Liz's was. He did not appear nervous, just pleased. "Hello, Elizabeth. How are you?" he asked, and when she said fine he allowed his gaze to go over to his wife.

"Elizabeth," he said to his wife, simply. Liz smiled at him and shook her head. "Here we go again." He retrieved her coat from the coat stand and helped her into it.

"Well, good luck," Elizabeth said. She felt very awkward standing there. "I'll hold down the fort."

"We'll call you," Liz said on her way out the door, Jack's hand on her back steering her out. She did not turn around. She had other things on her mind.

After they left, Elizabeth got some more paper towels, doused in warm water, and cleaned the stain on the carpet.

She was strangely nervous. *Amniotic fluid,* she thought. She remembered a time in seventh grade, when she had bled right through her gym uniform, leaving a small puddle of blood on the bleachers and a trail down her leg before another girl told her she was "leaking." How ashamed she had been, the whole gym class knowing that she, Elizabeth, "four-eyes", the teacher's pet (but not in gym), was having her period. It was unbearable, the embarrassment, the overly large underwear loaned from the nurse's office. Elizabeth had feigned vomiting so that her mother would come from work and pick her up.

There was no particular smell to the water from Liz's body, no flecks of blood. Elizabeth could have been cleaning up a spill from a vase of flowers.

Chapter 19

"It's a Girl"

The baby, Isabel Elise, was born sixteen hours after Liz left the office. Everything "came out just fine, wonderful," reported Jack when he called the next morning. "You're the third people—person—we've called," he said. "Our folks, first, of course."

"Well, I'm so happy for you," Elizabeth said. "A girl—that's so exciting."

"Yeah, well, Elizabeth was expecting a boy, and so, well, she's thrilled it's a girl. Tyler's pretty excited, too. If you want to visit at the hospital, I'm sure she'd be glad to see you."

"Oh, yes, I'll come by this evening." She had intended to visit at the hospital when the news was out, but it was still nice to be invited, to be on the list-to-be-called, like family. She hadn't expected to feel so pleased.

Isabel. It was a lovely name. Liz had not mentioned any possible names for a girl, since she had been so convinced it was another boy. All morning Elizabeth was consumed by thoughts of the new baby girl. At lunch she went to the mall and splurged on a tiny white jumper of fine cotton, a pink rattle, and some flowers for Liz. She left the package out, unwrapped, on her desk so that she could examine the delicate piping on the outfit in between packing boxes of magazines on grant writing and the eight lateral file drawers of old proposals.

She called her mother to tell her she would be late, and about Liz's baby.

"Girls are easier," said Mrs. Wright.

Elizabeth wondered how hard the labor had been, what it would feel like to have something so large coming out of you—not like menstrual blood—turning you inside out. She had seen a few birthing films in college and had a picture in her mind. For that matter, she wondered what it would feel like to have something growing inside of you... It was all quite natural, she chastised herself. Quite amazingly natural. And, at 50, not something she would ever experience. There had been a few years, in her late thirties, when Elizabeth had been depressed about this, about the way her life had turned out. Like her mother, she had always been a loner. And she did believe, as her mother did, that half—no, far more than half—of the people in the world weren't worth knowing anyway. And did she think that, out of that other half, she would actually meet someone compatible to spend her life with? Unlikely. And so there was no use, really, feeling depressed about it. That time had passed. She'd been involved with her work.

It was Thomas who suggested she take up ice skating again. Both of them had skated as children on the pond five blocks away. In Philadelphia, Thomas had joined a group of doctors who formed a hockey team down and played on the weekends. He really enjoyed it, and for her birthday ten years ago (which he usually forgot), he sent Elizabeth a generous gift certificate to a sports store that sold skates. She had gone and examined the skates, amazed at how expensive they were. She didn't use the gift certificate right away, choosing instead to go to the rink and rent skates.

She wouldn't forget that first time back on the ice. It had been so many years since she had skated. The rink was crowded, and normally Elizabeth would've waited for some other less busy time. But she made her way onto the rink, skating carefully twice around, arms out, her ankles wobbly. On the third cycle, she moved closer to the center where there was more room. She could feel the chill of the ice on her legs. She looked down at her white booted foot and the tight black pants she had bought for skating. The ice in the middle was still white and perfect and she watched her foot glide in front of her, and then the other, a bit faster. The curve and crossover came naturally.

She skated as long as she could, and by the end of the afternoon she felt she had found a bit of grace. She loved it.

Still, Elizabeth went for two more sessions before she began a thorough investigation of skates. And by the time of Thomas' next call, she had already purchased professional skates and was taking lessons. Thomas sounded surprised—impressed, even. And when he came up a few weeks later they went skating together. He even took her hands and skated backward to her forward, but they nearly collided with someone and skated independently after that. Then Thomas had broken his leg, and after that work got too busy, so he didn't skate anymore. Every year he asked Elizabeth about her skating, though.

Elizabeth pictured Liz going out the door yesterday, Jack's hand on the small of her back, that intimacy. Liz had gotten pregnant; they had "tried" to get pregnant for a while. She tried to imagine knowing you were going to have sex, over and over again, part of your daily life. What did they say to each other? "*Let's go do it?*" She pictured Liz's sturdy, ordinary body and Jack's....

These thoughts were ridiculous. Elizabeth called the hospital. Visiting hours were 4 to 6. She wrapped the baby smock in the mauve, floral wrapping she'd bought and decided to leave work early. However, just as she was packing to leave, Marjorie from Admissions poked her head in to inquire about Liz and, finding her gone, wanted to chat a while. Elizabeth told her how Liz had gone into labor in the office yesterday, and that she had had a little girl early this morning. "Oh! That is so exciting," Marjorie said in an exaggerated way (she had two grown sons), but she didn't sound the way Elizabeth was feeling.

Well, obviously, Marjorie hardly knew Liz.

And then Cathy DeFranco stopped by with a package from Lindell and, Elizabeth suspected, to check on the progress of packing-up. "How's everything going?" she asked, perky as ever. From behind Cathy's shoulder, Marjorie rolled her eyes at Elizabeth. Except for a monthly departmental meeting, Elizabeth hardly ever saw Cathy, who couldn't have been older than 26 and took great pride in her title of Director of Public Relations. Lindell liked her. Elizabeth had heard him say he "appreciated her energy." Lucky for her that her father was a good friend of the chairman of the Board of Trustees or she would not have the job. The college was throwing lots of money at public relations to keep its image looming in the local media, and Cathy still reported to a senior director who could save her when she ordered too much glossy stock.

"I would have sent my secretary over, but she was out today," Cathy smiled sweetly. That was another thing that rankled Elizabeth and proved how much money Administration was putting toward PR: Cathy, ridiculous little Cathy, had a full-time assistant. Rose, approaching retirement, was not the kind of assistant Elizabeth would want, but she bristled each time she heard Cathy call Rose "my secretary." In fact, she had never heard Cathy call Rose by her name.

"Where's *your* secretary?" Cathy looked around the half-packed room.

"Liz had a little girl this morning!" Marjorie piped up, stealing the story. Perhaps it was just as well, Elizabeth thought. Then those two could chit-chat about it and she could get to the hospital.

"*Really!*" Cathy exclaimed, pressing her hands together in a gesture both a clap and a prayer. "Oh, I'd like to have a baby girl." She straightened her suit. "Sometime." She said the word with both longing and efficiency, as if imagining the perfect years stretched out before her. Thank god her office was on the other side of the new suite, Elizabeth thought.

"Well, ladies, I have to go," she smiled.

"Congratulate her me for," Marjorie said. Cathy nodded in agreement, giving the room one last look so she could report to Lindell.

Elizabeth thought about the wet spot on the carpet where Liz's water had broken, almost dry now a day later. She would never say anything about it to anyone, even her mother. It was an intimacy between her and Liz.

Chapter 20

Isabel

Elizabeth stopped at the nursery window on her way to Liz's room and surveyed the newborns. There were about ten plexiglass tubs on rollers in the bright room. She squinted but couldn't see name tags. Most of the infants were swaddled tightly and sleeping, but on the right side of the room were two tubs under lamps, with tubes coming from them. These must be preemies. The nurse on duty smiled questioningly at her over a blue mask, but Elizabeth shook her head. She wasn't family.

At Liz's room, she paused. Liz was lying with the bed in a raised position, cradling the baby against her knees. Her face was pale, but content. Jack was in the bed next to her, one leg straddling on the floor. Together the three made a soft portrait. Elizabeth would have liked to have a photo of them to take out and examine later. "Oh, look!" Liz exclaimed at some movement of the baby. Then Jack saw Elizabeth and stood up to greet her.

"Hello, everyone," she said. "I hope I'm not interrupting."

Liz's hair was pulled back with a band. The dark circles under her eyes made her oddly radiant, someone Elizabeth had not seen before. Liz looked back at her blankly for a full second. "Oh, Elizabeth," she said, as though suddenly recognizing her, "Come and see Isabel."

Jack pulled up a chair for her close to the bed and Elizabeth tiptoed across the room, not liking the harsh sound her heels would make on the linoleum. The baby was starting to whimper.

"Jack, would you get me one of those diapers? I think this girl needs a change," Liz said, adjusting herself to a cross-legged position with a wince and putting the baby on the bed in front of her. Elizabeth watched as Liz unwrapped the baby of its tight flannel cloths. Its legs were so long and frog-like, the skin mottled and thin and new… She stared at the black tied-off stump at the infant's soon-to-become navel. The tiny chest with a ribcage that looked too large for it and the palest nipples. The baby's arms were clenched tight to its body. Liz untaped the diaper which looked hardly used, and the baby suddenly became a *she*, the vulva strangely enlarged compared to the rest of the body. Elizabeth watched as Liz quickly put on another huge diaper.

"It's the smallest size they make," Liz said, smiling at Elizabeth for the first time. "Want to hold her?"

Liz wrapped up the baby tightly and swiftly like a package, an expert again already, and Elizabeth awkwardly took her. She automatically bent to smell the baby, this girl Isabel, and closed her eyes in pleasure at the sweetness, the newness. She had not held a baby in years, since the previous neighbors had lived next door. The Picarillos were a young couple, and she was about five months pregnant when they moved in. Elizabeth, then 9, had watched them with great interest as Mrs. Picarillo's belly got larger and larger and then one evening they called Mrs. Wright and a week later they came home with Baby Molly. Elizabeth had gone over there every day after school, helping with housework or anything that

Mrs. Picarillo might need in exchange for a chance to hold that baby. The smell came back to her now.

Jack and Liz were talking quietly about something—arrangements to get out of the hospital, something about how long her mother would be staying… Elizabeth stood up with the baby and walked in a small circle on the other side of the room to give them some privacy. Carefully she shifted the baby to her shoulder and back again. How light, how like nothing, this package of human bones and flesh. *Isabel.*

"Oh, you baby girl," she said, and stroked the baby's face with the side of her finger. The baby's face crinkled and she coughed a little and pursed her lips. Elizabeth stroked her again and her small tongue came out. She made another coughing noise, the beginning of crying. Elizabeth felt herself begin to perspire in her suit.

"Elizabeth, I think she wants to eat," Liz said, and Elizabeth returned the baby to her.

"Should I leave you all alone?" Elizabeth inquired.

"Oh, no—not unless you have to go," Liz said. "We haven't even opened your gift." Elizabeth had put the gift at the end of the bed when she came in. "Open it, Jack," Liz said. She had discreetly lifted her gown and Elizabeth glanced sideways long enough to glimpse a large pink nipple going into the baby's mouth.

"Oh, it's beautiful," Liz said as Jack held up the baby outfit. "Of course, she'll probably spit up all over it."

"I'm afraid it's much too large," Elizabeth commented.

"Oh, don't worry," Jack said. "She'll be in it in no time."

Elizabeth stayed a few more minutes, long enough for Liz to switch breasts. Elizabeth was vaguely embarrassed, and embarrassed again at feeling that way. Breastfeeding was a natural thing, after all, and the best thing for the baby; that was clearly documented. Perhaps it was just the strangeness of it, of knowing Liz and yet not knowing her...

She took her leave at the appropriate moment. She said she missed Liz at the office and hoped that she and the baby would visit soon. They'd be in the new space. Liz thanked her for the gift.

As she started her car in the hospital parking lot, Elizabeth remembered the Picarillo's again. How one evening she'd watched them from her window: Mr. Picarillo unbuttoning his shirt and Mrs. Picarillo coming up, hugging him from behind. Elizabeth had watched as Mrs. Picarillo's hand went down around him, to his pants, and they had both stood there a moment and then he had turned around and put his hand on her breast, squeezing it and squeezing it in a nasty way and then he had done something with her dress, lifted it up and fumbled and then her hands were around his neck, her legs around him and they were jerking together like they were in some kind of fit and then Mr. Picarillo had carried his wife away from the view, leaving Elizabeth breathless and estranged at her own window. She'd known, of course, that this was how babies were made. And although she knew that Mr. and Mrs. Picarillo were married, she could not look at Mrs. Picarillo's clear smiling face the same way anymore after that. The Picarillos had had five boys in the six years after that. Elizabeth had not cared about the boys the way she loved Baby Molly. Then the Picarillos had moved away. Mrs. Wright had been glad. "Those boys would've been a nuisance," she'd said.

Elizabeth pulled into the driveway and looked at the neighbor's tidy house with the white vinyl siding. She wondered where all the Picarillos were today. Mrs. Picarillo would be 70-ish, and did she remember her young married days?

Chapter 21

Expectations

Because they paid cash, each month Elizabeth had to personally collect the rent from the Phans. She would try to call ahead, but they rarely answered the phone. She wondered if it was a cultural thing, not answering the phone. She would drive over around dinnertime. It was dark by then. "Be careful," her mother said to her each time as she left after an early dinner.

In December and January she had had to make two trips, since they weren't home. The big old blue Impala was not here today, either. Elizabeth sighed and pulled up to the front curb. Both Maureen, the real estate agent, and Mr. Phan had mentioned to her that the Phans had cousins who were looking for a place to live, and Maureen thought that might be a good way to rent out the lower floor and attic. Elizabeth wasn't so sure it was a good idea. When she had told Mr. Phan about the cable coming out of the bedroom he had been sulky, almost recalcitrant. The next time she'd come by the hole was still there, but the cable was gone. And now, of course, the hole would have to be patched. His other relatives weren't likely to be more cooperative.

Nevertheless, she turned off her engine and went up to the middle apartment to look around. The rattling keys made a hollow sound in the empty main room, which was a duplicate of the room upstairs. Elizabeth took off her shoes and went from room to room in the apartment, turning on lights and turning them off again, as if looking for something. Under the bright overhead lights the rooms were quiet and dusty. Back in the front room, she unlatched a window to air the place out. When she turned around, she couldn't believe she hadn't seen it when she first came in: a small puddle of water right in the center of the room. The hardwood was already beginning to turn black. Elizabeth looked up to the source of the water and saw a large brown circle in the plaster overhead. The overhead light was just inches away from the circle and Elizabeth quickly turned it off in fear of a short-out or fire.

What were they doing up there? The wave of irritation that she felt was so strong that if there were a chair in the room, she would have sat down to recover. She heard car doors slamming downstairs and went to the window to see Mr. Phan and his wife looking at her car parked in front of the house. Mrs. Phan said something and Mr. Phan shrugged. The kids were already clambering up the stairs. She could hear the sharp sounds of Vietnamese as they probably tried to figure out where she was. Since the grandmother hadn't gotten out of the car, it occurred to Elizabeth that she might have been in the apartment the whole time, as she had been that time Elizabeth was raking in the backyard.

She waited until she was sure they were all upstairs before she went up. She knocked on the door. The talking stopped abruptly; there was some more sharp whispering, and finally Mr. Phan opened the door just as Elizabeth was about to knock again. From over Mr. Phan's shoulder she immediately saw the cause of the water damage: the white plastic bird bath that had been missing from the yard for two months stood like an urn on the rice paper mat in the center of the living room. For two months Mr. Phan had come downstairs to deliver the rent money; now she knew why.

Beyond the birdbath the grandmother sat on the couch in the same black polyester slacks and red sweater Elizabeth had seen her in when they first moved in. It was as though the woman had never moved.

"Mr. Phan," Elizabeth said, "come with me please." She turned sharply so that he would not have a chance to equivocate and led him to the downstairs apartment where she showed him the water damage the birdbath had caused.

"Oh," Mr. Phan nodded, "oh." He nodded again, but there was no sign of understanding on his face. In fact, he smiled.

"Mr. Phan," she said, "I have no idea why you *took* my birdbath from the yard and put it in your living room, much less why you filled it with water, but it has already caused damage."

"What you call it?" he asked.

"A birdbath. A *bird bath*, for *birds*. It belongs outside. This is unacceptable."

He shrugged. "The grandmother see it. She not used to sink with handles." He made a twisting movement with his hand, as though turning on a faucet.

"She *washes* in the bird bath?" Elizabeth was incredulous.

He shrugged again, bit his lip and looked at the floor. Obviously, he wanted to get out of here. What did he expect her to do? Just go along with it and watch her apartments become ruined?

"Well, it must be emptied and removed. Let's go; I'll help you."

Mr. Phan hesitated, then followed her out the door and waited while she locked the lower apartment. Upstairs, Elizabeth examined the water in the bird bath, which was gray and filmy and probably a respiratory health hazard.

"Do you have a pot?" she asked. "We can use a pot to get most of the water out and then empty the rest."

Mr. Phan said something sharply to his wife and she produced a saucepan. Elizabeth scooped a pan full of water and, double-handed, took it to the sink while Mr. Phan stood awkwardly in the kitchen doorway. Obviously, he was going to be no help. On the second trip to the sink Elizabeth kicked off her shoes. After five trips, she and Mr. Phan awkwardly lugged the top bowl of the bird bath into the kitchen. As she saw what was happening, the grandmother made a hissing noise and starting yelling something. Elizabeth paused and looked across the bird bath at Mr. Phan, whose face was red with either exertion or embarrassment at the whole situation. He yelled something at his wife, who went over to her mother and tried to settle her. Elizabeth heard a brief struggle behind her, but she and Mr. Phan made it to the sink and emptied the last of the water.

The base of the birdbath was supposed to be weighted down with a bag of sand or concrete, but the Phan's had not done that. It was a miracle that the huge bowl of water hadn't toppled over.

She squatted down in her suit and rolled up the rice paper matting, revealing a damp floor and a huge black water stain. "You see?" she said in an elementary voice toward the grandmother. Elizabeth finally looked over at the couch, where Mrs. Phan sat on one side of her mother and Lucy sat on the other. She hadn't noticed Lucy slip into the room.

Lucy was looking at her, frightened at the scene and crying silently, clinging to her grandmother's arm. The grandmother's wrinkled cheeks were sucked in tight and she glared straight ahead as if catatonic. Elizabeth could feel the gaze of the other two children, who watched silently from the hallway.

"You will please help me take this down to the basement," Elizabeth said, realizing her syntax was beginning to match Mr. Phan's. She slipped her shoes back on and hung her bag on her shoulder.

Without water, the plastic parts were light. She carried the base; Mr. Phan struggled with the bowl and they took the birdbath to the cellar, where Elizabeth stowed it under the worktable and locked the cellar door. On another weekend she could retrieve it and take it to Milport.

She brushed the dirt off her hands. She parted company with Mr. Phan on the porch—why did they never turn the light on? "I will be requiring the rent next week," she said to him. He nodded. "I'm sorry to have disturbed your mother-in-law," she said, "but some things just aren't acceptable. This was my aunt's place."

Perhaps he didn't understand her English. Mr. Phan's face remained inscrutable, and she left him that way on the porch. Before she fell asleep that night, Elizabeth went over the scenario in her head several times: finding the puddle, the Phan's arrival, emptying the birdbath bowl, the grandmother's yells, Lucy's frightened face, and Mr. Phan's silhouette on the porch. Lucy's face bothered her the most. Should she not have been so harsh?

It hadn't been a good situation, and that was that. There was nothing more to be done except make sure he understood her expectations.

Chapter 22

Valentine's Brunch

Elizabeth invited Liz and the baby for brunch on Valentine's Day, a Sunday. She and her mother hadn't had company in a long time, and Elizabeth spent Saturday afternoon decorating the house. She even made a couple of trips to the drugstore for doilies, paper hearts and some candy, which she put out in small dishes in the living room and on the dining room table.

"I don't know what all this fuss is about," said Mrs. Wright. "She's not your boyfriend."

Elizabeth ignored her. She enjoyed getting ready. This would be a party for just the girls. On the phone she had apologized to Liz about not inviting Jack. Liz scoffed and said Jack probably had something else going on, or he would sleep in, since Isabel had been keeping them up nights.

Elizabeth wanted to do the cooking and ousted her mother from the kitchen. As she made coffee and mixed an egg batter for French toast, Elizabeth realized she would be very glad to have some company again in the office. She had hoped that Liz would be able to come in a few times while on maternity leave and visit with the baby, and maybe even run some of those reports that Elizabeth was having a hard time getting out of the machine. With pay, of course. She could watch the baby while Liz worked—that wouldn't be a problem. But Liz had not come in, and Elizabeth knew she would be out of line in asking her. Next week, though, Liz would be back officially, coming in during the afternoons, like before.

"When is your secretary coming back?" Cathy DeFranco had asked at the copy machine last week. Elizabeth loved Institutional Advancement's copier with its sort and staple and hole-punch options. She did not, however, like the way that just standing there was an invitation to be interrupted.

"She'll be back in a couple of weeks."

"Oh." Cathy sighed. "I think I'd *die* if I didn't have my secretary for six weeks." She stood sloppily, one hand folded back on her hip. She wore a perfect (Elizabeth had yet to see her in the same suit twice) cream-colored wool suit that set off her auburn hair.

"Well, one has to get organized," Elizabeth said and went back to her office.

At the new site, she kept her door closed most of the time. At least that way every Tom, Dick, and Harry wouldn't pop his head in to examine the space. Cathy's comment had annoyed her. Why did Cathy have a full-time assistant, and why was that issue always a struggle for Elizabeth with administration? How hard she'd had to fight just to formally hire a *part-time* assistant. She knew that life was not fair. With Cathy's connections, Elizabeth also knew that unless Cathy got married *and* pregnant, she wasn't going anywhere, so there was no use gyrating about her.

Elizabeth could, however, begin again to make a case for a full-time assistant position. Perhaps someone to supplement Liz, in the mornings. Or, maybe in a few months after the baby was settled, Liz would come on full-time. There was plenty to do—there *could* be plenty to do. She was thinking this when she heard Liz's car pull into the driveway (she'd told her to drive right in and park behind her car).

"She's here. *Now* will you let me do this?" Mrs. Wright said irritably, coming from the living room where she had been trying to read the paper, but was probably worrying that Elizabeth was burning her good pan. "Here, give me that," she said, as Elizabeth removed her apron.

Liz was looking over the back fence at the yard, the bassinet with Isabel casually over her arm like a huge basket of flowers or fruit. "Here, let me help you with that," Elizabeth called.

"She's dead asleep," Liz said, handing over the heavy bassinet. "And that's fine with me."

"Isabel!" Elizabeth sang out to the sleeping baby. The day was oddly warm for a clear day in February. "It's a good day," she said cheerfully. This must be how grandparents feel, she thought. Anticipation, arrival, all that perfect innocence for a delimited period of time.

"It must be a good day," Liz teased her. "You've got *slacks* on."

Inside, Mrs. Wright greeted Liz and quickly turned back to the French toast. "We're leaving the baby with you," Elizabeth said, placing Isabel carefully on the dining room table amidst the doilies and heart candy. "I'm giving Liz the tour."

"I can probably handle that," Mrs. Wright said.

"*White* carpet!" Liz exclaimed at the front room.

"Don't blame me for that!" Mrs. Wright called out.

"She loves it," whispered Elizabeth.

Liz followed her from room to room, exclaiming at this and that, and Elizabeth felt very pleased and girlish. Since she had moved back in with her mother, every room had been redone at least once, even though the bedrooms were small. Every time she went into her room, she was satisfied again at the floral green and blue fabric of the canopy and duvet on her bed, and the matching print along the top edge of the walls. That project had taken four months to complete. It was that satisfaction, she thought, that made the time and energy and expense worthwhile.

"Since you grew up in this house, don't you sometimes feel weirded-out?" Liz asked. "I mean, this is the house of your *childhood*."

Elizabeth shrugged. "Not really. It's a different house." The house of her "childhood" was in her memory, not in this physical space. She had had the same room, but the floor had been scuffed hardwood (even as a girl she'd hated that floor), and she'd had a rickety twin bed facing the other direction. The smallest room had been Thomas', which was now the study with those glass bookcases from Ethan Allen. And the downstairs had been completely rearranged. The only room that had remained the same was her mother's bedroom: a simple double bed and nightstand on a plain rug. Mrs. Wright had allowed Elizabeth to have a full-length closet installed in the room, since they were short of storage space in the house, but she had not let her have carpeting put in. "I don't need it," she said.

Elizabeth took her to the basement so show her the new energy-saving washer and dryer set she'd bought (Jack had recommended the brand). Since her patterns in the basement usually involved a beeline to the laundry and back, Elizabeth hadn't noticed how packed the basement had gotten. Thomas had left several boxes of books with them the last time he changed apartments and hadn't retrieved them yet. They made a wall in the middle of the room that Elizabeth and her mother circled around when they did laundry. Mrs. Wright usually washed the few items that didn't go to the dry cleaner's, and Elizabeth saw Liz glance sideways at several pairs of her full-brief panties pinned on a line over the washer.

"Let's eat!" Mrs. Wright called from upstairs.

"God, she's going to wake Isabel if she yells like that," Elizabeth muttered.

"Don't worry about it." Liz touched her shoulder.

Isabel was still sleeping sweetly when they sat down to eat, and Liz moved to put the bassinet on the floor beside her, but Elizabeth demanded that she leave Isabel on the dining table. "That way it's like she's eating with us, too. Plus, there might be a draft on the floor."

Liz smiled and shrugged. "Whatever you say, boss."

Elizabeth served the French toast, sprinkling powdered sugar over each plate and warming the syrup in the microwave. The meal was quiet. They discussed the value of real maple syrup versus the corn-syrup variety. Elizabeth maintained that it was both more delicious and healthier.

"And five times more expensive," Mrs. Wright said.

"It doesn't really make that much difference, does it?" said Liz.

Mrs. Wright asked Liz about childcare arrangements when she went back to work. "Oh, I think we're pretty much set," Liz said. "I'll be home in the mornings, like before, and Jack's mother will come over after lunch. We need the benefits at the college. They've got good medical for me and the kids." Liz had finished her sausage and French toast, and Elizabeth offered her the last piece. She hadn't cooked in a long time, and her mother never ate much, so she hadn't known what to prepare. She recalled that nursing mothers ate more.

After they had finished, as if on cue, Isabel began to fuss. "She must have smelled the French toast," Elizabeth said.

Liz took her out of the bassinet.

"Mother, isn't she beautiful?" Elizabeth exclaimed.

"She's beautifully quiet," said Mrs. Wright, who seemed oddly embarrassed. "Why don't you two go visit in the other room and let me clean up here?"

"I need to feed her," Liz said. "Where should I go?"

"The study would probably be good," Elizabeth said. "Do you mind if I come, too?"

"No, sure."

As she escorted Liz back upstairs with the fussing baby, Elizabeth felt foolish. Liz could have comfortably nursed Isabel right there in the living room. It wasn't as if there were any men around. But the study would be cozy.

Elizabeth retrieved a couple of pillows from her room and watched intently from a respectful distance as Liz set herself up, putting Isabel down beside her on the small couch as she unhooked one cup of her nursing bra. Then she scooped the crying baby up, lifted her shirt and pressed a nipple into its mouth in one smooth motion. Elizabeth looked at Liz's face, which was at that moment completely attentive to the baby, making faces at her. Elizabeth came closer and sat down on the couch. Over the mound of pulled-up shirt, Isabel was awake while latched on to the breast, looking very matter-of-factly at her mother and then her gaze strayed over to Elizabeth and then back to Liz. Liz's nipples must be twice their normal size. The pink rim of the aureola was still visible.

Elizabeth knew this was natural, but there was something grotesque about it. Isabel unlatched from Liz for a moment, and thin yellow milk leaked from both the breast and the baby's mouth.

"Okay, other side," Liz said, unhooking the other nursing cup and pressing a cloth diaper to her other breast to dry it. Isabel made little grunting noises as she sucked.

"Does it hurt?"

"Maybe a little at first, but, no, mostly it feels good. It's the best thing for them, you know. And it's the easiest."

"I've heard that."

"Tyler likes to watch me feed the baby. I think he likes to think about himself doing it when he was a baby."

Elizabeth had actually forgotten about Liz's other child. "So none of this is new to you," she said.

"Not new, no, but it's different. She…I don't know. She responds more."

Isabel made little chirping noises as she nursed. Outside, the gray sky was clearing. From downstairs, they could hear water running as the dishes were washed. Mrs. Wright had the radio on, which was rare—something classical—and if they strained, they could hear an off-key tone as she hummed along.

Recognizing this at the same time, Elizabeth and Liz looked at each other and smiled.

Chapter 23

A Good Day

For a couple of weeks in May, Jack's mother was out of town and Elizabeth saw the baby every day when Liz brought Isabel to work for half an hour or so before Jack came to pick her up. Isabel had gotten so big! Elizabeth remembered reading about the exponential growth of infants during the first two years after birth in a nutrition class way back when, but it was still startling to see a *person* evolving from that tiny bundle she'd seen at the hospital six months ago.

The previous week, on Elizabeth's birthday, Liz had baked a cake and Jack brought Isabel in for a visit after lunch. Elizabeth found herself flushed and near tears at the surprise. She was now 53, a rather anticlimactic year. She and her mother had planned to go out for dinner at a new Italian place in downtown Milport, and later in the week Sahil said he'd take her out—for Chinese, most likely.

They took Isabel into Elizabeth's larger office, closed the outer door, spread the blanket out on the floor and put her down. Elizabeth took off her shoes and got down on the floor with her. Isabel was at her best, chortling, tugging at the folds of her dress, a beautiful hand-sewn pink frock with white piping around the collar.

"I wanted to dress her up for your birthday," Liz said. "I knew you'd like it. Jack's mom made the dress."

The baby had been in to visit before, and Elizabeth loved to watch her position herself on all fours in her miniature sweatsuit and rock back and forth, as though getting ready for some kind of broad jump. Then she'd pivot to a sitting position, a little buddha, and let out a shriek, grin at the sound of her own voice, and shriek again.

They had cake. Liz invited a couple other people from the office—Lindell, Tom Murphy, and Ann Lupinsky—for a piece of cake. Elizabeth had told no one about her birthday, but they all laughed to see her on the floor with Isabel and wished her well as though they had known. After a while Jack had to go, and they packed Isabel into her bassinet like a machine with many parts and off they went.

That was a good day.

On other days during the week without a babysitter Elizabeth held the baby while Liz got settled and turned on her computer and looked at her email. Then she came in and scooped Isabel up to feed her before Jack came by. "I left him a bottle in the freezer," Liz said, "but god knows if he'll remember to tell the sitter about it." She seemed exasperated by the arrangements while Jack's mother was not around. She nursed Isabel in her office chair while she talked to Elizabeth. From across the room, Elizabeth could see Liz's white midriff where her shirt was pulled up.

One time, Elizabeth feigned needing a book that was in the case behind Liz so that she could come closer and see Isabel's face as she nursed. Isabel sucked peacefully, casually, eyes open, amiably squeezing Liz's shirt and trying to pat her face with her free left hand, and then looking up over Liz's shoulder to Elizabeth. She unlatched from the breast for a moment in interest, and milk dripped on her face, and then she went back to her feeding, her eyes looking over Liz's shoulder and fixing on Elizabeth.

"It's strange," Liz said, out of nowhere. "This baby-feeding."

It was odd she said that, because Elizabeth was wondering at just that moment what it felt like to nurse a baby, to have some tiny creature *on* you, drawing from you. No one had ever sucked on her breasts. Nor, she thought, would she want them to—least of all a man. Although, if she had a child, she would probably nurse it. It was much healthier and promoted good bonding... There were dark hairs around Liz's large nipples. Apparently she didn't bother to pluck them out, as Elizabeth did. It embarrassed her to even think about it so specifically. Plucking the hairs was just part of personal hygiene. She didn't like how they looked.

Then Jack came in, looking rushed and rather handsome as he took the satiated baby, stopping to change Isabel's diapers before he left, and bundling her up and slinging her lovingly over his shoulder, casually, like a favorite sweater. "Bye-bye!" Liz and Elizabeth called to Isabel as they left out the back way.

Then Liz and Elizabeth went back to work, awkwardly going back to their separate offices. It was half an hour before Elizabeth could concentrate again.

Chapter 24

Full-Time Support

Finally, Administration approved a full-time assistant position, but it took more than two weeks before Elizabeth could bring the subject up to Liz. She wasn't sure exactly why she was hesitant. Having two part-time assistants would be awkward administratively; there would be all kinds of details to be ironed out about who did what. There would also have to be some arrangement about the number of hours, since there was only one benefits package with the position and Liz purposefully worked the minimum number of hours she had to in order to get the medical insurance.

What she really wanted was for Liz to take the job full-time. Sometimes she had the sense that Liz would like the extra money, and she'd been so helpful on those days where she worked all day to help her get out one of Sahil's grants. When Elizabeth had complained that, despite her success, she still didn't have a full-time support position, Liz had nodded empathetically but made no comment.

And, actually, to be a *good* full-time job, the responsibilities would have to be expanded, Elizabeth mused. Perhaps there could be more outreach to faculty, or grant-writing training seminars (of which she'd done a few when she first came on board, but that had fallen off the past several years). Of course, all this would require some training, but Liz might be capable of it.... The bottom line was that the position had been approved. Whether Liz wanted it or not was up to her. If she didn't, perhaps her other half would be interested in working with the faculty. Elizabeth let out a sigh. Thinking about working with faculty made her tired. She decided to approach the subject with Liz before she left that night.

She heard Liz talking to someone in the other room, a brief laugh, and a moment later she saw Tom Murphy, the new prospect research person, walk down the hall. Now that Liz had been back for a couple of months, the new recruits were making themselves known. Elizabeth wished Liz would use the back entrance, as she herself did, so there wasn't such a hubbub with Lindell's drones.

At five o'clock, Elizabeth heard Liz getting ready to go and she went into her office. "You know, Liz, I've been meaning to tell you, but with the baby visiting this week and all…"

Liz looked at her inquiringly.

She hadn't meant to bring the baby into it. In fact, she hadn't thought about what Liz would do with Isabel if she were to go full-time. Elizabeth winced inside and plunged ahead.

"I've got the go-ahead for a full-time position, and I just wanted to let you know first, before I go searching for your complement, in case you're interested in working full-time." She smiled at Liz. "Your work is really excellent, I feel. You bring a lot to the job."

Liz was biting her lip and frowning slightly. "Well, thank you. I didn't… well, you *did* say you were thinking about this being a full-time…"

"You really don't have to make up your mind this minute. Take a week or so. There's a lot to discuss."

"Well, okay." Now Liz's lips were pursed and she was gazing at her desk.

Elizabeth hesitated. "Do you have any questions?"

Liz looked at her. "Well, it's not a question, really, just a thought. I'm just not sure the assistant job really *is* a full-time job. I mean, I'm not sure what I or someone else would do for those other hours."

Elizabeth's mouth tightened. "Well, actually, there's a *lot* that can be done that I'm taking care of that I'd like to pass on. And beyond that, I'm thinking of ways to expand the job to serve more of the faculty. So, if you're interested, I offer the extra hours to you. Just let me know."

Liz met her eyes and then looked down again, slightly flushed. "Okay, I'll think about it. I'll talk to Jack."

Elizabeth smiled at her to relieve some of the tension. Of course, she thought, in her four hours per day Liz wouldn't really have a complete sense of all the functions of the Grants Office. Elizabeth had continued to do many of the menial tasks she was accustomed to doing, not having ever had a dependable, full-time assistant. There was much to think about and plans to be made. And even though she was surprised at Liz's initial hesitant response, she still hoped she would take the job.

Chapter 25

Road Trips

Elizabeth had decided to purchase a new car. She liked her Acura, but it was over 10 years old and beginning to need more repairs. She had also just received her annual raise and it felt like time to treat herself. She thought about it for several weeks and researched a few other kinds of cars online before she actually went to the dealer. She didn't want a new brand, just a new model.

She and her mother had gone out for a long drive with the salesman, Mrs. Wright riding in the backseat, looking disinterestedly out the window while the salesman prompted Elizabeth to try the navigation system, the sunroof, seat warmer, and accelerating onto the highway.

"Really, Elizabeth, it feels just like the old one to me. I don't see why we—excuse me, *you*—need to get a new car," Mrs. Wright said as they pulled back into the sales lot. Elizabeth knew she wanted a Acura, but she didn't think it would look good to be too eager or straightforward with the salesmen, and she enjoyed looking around, sitting in the various models. They had been at the dealer's for over an hour before Elizabeth found the right car to test drive, and her mother was grouchy. Since Mrs. Wright had asked to come along, Elizabeth did not feel like coddling her through the choosing of the car. She would take as much time as needed.

"It feels entirely different, mother," she said when the salesman got out of the car. "It's much tighter, the driver's seat is much more comfortable and it handles beautifully." What could her mother say to that? She had stopped driving five years ago when her vision got bad, and depended on Elizabeth and a couple of friends to take her to the grocery store and run errands. "And the old one doesn't have GPS, which I could really use." This was not entirely true, as she rarely had off-campus appointments, and she and her mother hadn't taken a road trip in over a year.

For a while, years ago after she first got her job at the college, she and her mother would take week-long road trips for her vacation. Elizabeth protested to Marjorie and others that this was just one of the obligations of caring for one's aging mother, but she actually enjoyed the trips. Often they would start with a visit to her brother in Philadelphia and then go someplace from there. They went to Amish country, and to the Hershey chocolate factory. Another time they drove to Washington, DC, and visited a couple of sites there. The excursion to Maine was a good one, too. They were good traveling companions, quiet for hours, enjoying the same food and the same sites. Elizabeth liked to poke around in shops more than her mother, who would sit on a bench somewhere nearby and watch people. Mrs. Wright always insisted on paying for half of the trip.

"You've got your own retirement to think of," she would say. Elizabeth did not disagree, although her financial planner had told her she would be in very good shape to retire well before she was 67.

Last year they'd planned a long weekend to visit an historic colonial village nearby and shop in the outlet stores on the way home but it rained in a downpour all day. Mrs. Wright wasn't feeling well, and so they came home a day early. Elizabeth missed her shopping; Mrs. Wright complained about everything all the way home, and both were glad when they finally pulled into their driveway.

There were no other road trips last year, and they hadn't spoken of one this summer. Elizabeth looked across the dealer floor at her mother, sitting on the couch in front of the lobby TV. The navy sweater and slacks Elizabeth had bought her at Christmas hung on her slender frame. For the first time, Elizabeth thought she looked her age, 77. As if sensing she was being watched, Mrs. Wright looked over at Elizabeth and called out loudly, "We need to get going. The washer man was supposed to come between 2 and 4."

Elizabeth turned away. She'd decided she'd buy the car they'd test driven. It was gold with tan leather interior, and all the extras she normally wouldn't pay much attention to, but the purchase would be easy and she suddenly didn't want to think about it anymore. "I'll think about it," she said to the salesman. She would call him in a couple of days and see if she could improve the off-the-lot price.

Chapter 26

There You Have It

On Saturday afternoon Mrs. Wright made soup as she usually did, and Elizabeth worked outside on her hands and knees in the hydrangea bushes, clearing out the dead sticks and leaves. She'd hoped to complete the task in the morning, but at noon she was tired and hungry and knew it would take another day.

"Well, I cleared most of it," she said as she came in for lunch. To have half the yard clean and cleared and the other half in disarray felt like a bad itch.

"That's good." Her mother was rinsing out the sink.

"I wish I was done. It's annoying."

Her mother hummed a little tune. "You keep wishing it would be done—if it was all *done*, you'd be dead."

"Geez, Mother."

After lunch, Elizabeth went into the living room and plopped down on the couch in front of the television. It was going to be a lazy afternoon, she decided. She unhooked her bra from inside her shirt, as she usually did coming home from work, extracted it gracefully through her sleeve and threw it across the room to the base of the stairs. A rerun of "Beauty and the Beast" was on television and she felt suddenly very content to be in the company of Catherine and Vincent and their romantic partnership against crime and evil. When the television series had originally come out in the 1980s she had gotten hooked and planned that particular

116

weeknight around the show. Her mother had joined her for one episode. "Hogwash," she'd said, simply. Elizabeth remembered this now and smiled.

"What's this? Too lazy to get up the stairs?" Mrs. Wright said, retrieving the bra from the landing. "I'm going up for a nap."

Elizabeth also fell asleep on the couch and awoke in the late afternoon to a whimpering sound. At first she thought she herself had made the noise; then she thought it was coming from outside—the neighbor's cat, perhaps. After a few moments, she slowly realized the sound was coming from her mother's room upstairs.

She went up and found Mrs. Wright curled on her side, asleep, one arm covering her head as if hiding. The mewing noise was so unlike her that Elizabeth felt panicked.

"Mother?" She came over and put her hand tentatively on her mother's shoulder.

Mrs. Wright shot up suddenly, disoriented, and Elizabeth pulled back. "Were you having a nightmare, Mother?"

Mrs. Wright turned toward her with an intense look so angry that Elizabeth recoiled further. "I tell you…I tell you! Your father was a drunk and a beater, and it's a good thing— a *good* thing—he died when he did." She was breathing heavily and her fists were clenched. "Why do you think I can hardly hear out of this ear?" She cupped her right ear.

What was she talking about? Was she still asleep? Was she having a stroke? Elizabeth wondered, her heart racing.

Mrs. Wright' eyes grew softer but did not change their focus on Elizabeth's face. "There you have it. *There*," she said, and leaned back on the pillows. Elizabeth stood up so her mother could swing her legs back onto the bed. They looked at each other for several seconds. She did not know what to say, and covered her mother with the throw.

"Are you feeling alright? Can I get you anything?"

"I feel fine. I'm just tired." Mrs. Wright closed her eyes.

Elizabeth waited outside the door for a few minutes, in case her mother had not really fallen back asleep, then went downstairs slowly, letting the outburst sink in. Her father had beaten her mother? Elizabeth knew very little about him. There was the photo on her mother's bureau of the two of them just after their civil marriage ceremony, awkwardly holding hands, a full two feet of space between them. He was big and blonde and American, in sharp contrast to his bride, thin and foreign-looking, like she'd just gotten off the boat, which she had, only six months previous.

Elizabeth had gotten so used to not having a father that she rarely thought of him. Mrs. Wright never told any stories about him. They had been married for six years, and when Thomas was five and she was an infant, he had died of pneumonia. Aunt May had filled in as a partner to her mother right from the beginning. At family dinners, the two of them would exchange looks when Thomas, usually, would ask a question about their father, and May or her mother would offer a quick, snap-shut answer. Eventually, Thomas stopped asking about him.

Her mother had always been hard of hearing in her right ear.

Elizabeth found herself in the kitchen. It was getting dark; she turned on the overhead light and stirred the soup. If what her mother had said wasn't just part of a dream, made-up, she now had more information about her father, and Elizabeth realized she didn't want it. How could she not be interested?

she wondered. But she wasn't. He was gone. Her father's life was a sealed box that she'd never had access to.

She was worried, of course, about her mother. The clock on the wall ticked loudly in the quiet room. Elizabeth sighed. She heard movement overhead and in a few moments Mrs. Wright made her way downstairs, grabbing her apron off the hook without missing a step as she came into the kitchen. She looked her usual self and took the spoon from Elizabeth's hand.

"Mother," she said carefully. "That was quite a dream you were having."

"It was." Mrs. Wright pursed her lips, looking into the soup pot. "It's true, you know. All that."

Elizabeth hesitated. "Mother, do you need to talk about this?" Her voice sounded high and frightened, like a girl's.

"No. I'm fine," Mrs. Wright said, looking her daughter in the eye. "That's all done with. No need to talk about it."

Chapter 27

A Quick Tour

Elizabeth made a point of going by her aunt's building once a week to keep an eye on the place after the incident with the bird bath. As the days got longer she usually went after work. Once, when Liz's car was being serviced, Elizabeth gave her a ride home in her new Acura and stopped on the way to give her a quick tour. She found herself oddly excited to show off the new car, opening the sun roof to let in the early summer air.

"It's nice, Elizabeth."

The Phans were home when they came by. There were three late model cars parked in front of the house. Good, Elizabeth thought. Let them think I'm showing the apartment to a prospective buyer. Or renter.

She showed Liz through the vacant apartment.

"You see the mess," Elizabeth noted, talking somewhat louder than usual, pointing to the still blackened spot in the center of the main room.

"It's pretty weird, a bird bath in your living room," Liz agreed, hands stuffed in her coat pockets, but didn't say anything else. Granted, Liz had heard the story told to both Marjorie and Sahil. But since she'd begun working full-time three months ago, Liz seemed a bit more reticent than before, quieter. She was up from her desk a lot. Sometimes Elizabeth would hear her laugh in the hallway, but when Liz was back in her office she was quiet again, no evidence of a joke. Now that the baby was in daycare full-time Liz didn't bring her in very often. Elizabeth wondered whether something was going on at home, if she and Jack were having problems.

Elizabeth took her to the backyard. On two evenings after work last week she had cleared out leaves and twigs and trash from the flower beds that ran along three sides of the fence. "There used to be roses along this fence," she said. "My aunt was a good gardener and kept the soil loose and composted."

"Oh," Liz replied.

At home, her mother kept charge of the flower beds, and she didn't relish any interference, so Elizabeth generally left it to her, taking her to Home Depot or the garden shop for supplies. But this place could use a little color, Elizabeth thought. She didn't think she'd be up to the maintenance or expense of roses, but today she thought she might plant some impatiens in the side beds. It was still a little early in the season, but perhaps by next week—purple and white.

They were at the end of the plain rectangular yard and turned to look at the back of the building. It looked good, but in another year or so it would need repainting. Grass was beginning to sprout in the circle in the middle of the yard where the birdbath had been.

Suddenly in the window she was startled by a face—a plain, white face with dark hair and no expression—and just as suddenly the face was gone, as if she had been jerked out of the window frame.

"Lucy!" she said.

"What?" Liz asked.

"I just saw their little girl, the Phans' little girl, Lucy. And then she just disappeared."

They both gazed at the window. There was no sign of any movement. Was Lucy okay? Elizabeth wondered. Shouldn't she be in school? Then she realized that it was the end of the day. And Lucy, if she *was* in kindergarten, would have gotten out of school in the early afternoon.

But why didn't she smile, or wave? And why did she disappear so quickly? Elizabeth wondered whether she should think of an excuse to knock on the Phans' door.

She would have spoken of these worries to Liz, but Liz seemed elsewhere. "I should probably get home," Liz said.

"Yes, of course."

Chapter 28

Impatiens

Two weeks later, Elizabeth left work a bit early one day, went home to change her clothes, lined the trunk and backseat of her car with plastic garbage bags, then drove to Home Depot to buy ten flats of impatiens. She would keep it simple, planting the whole yard in impatiens, one side at a time. She didn't know exactly how many flats it would take, but it didn't matter; she could return as many times as necessary to the store and just leave the plastic bags in the car in the interim.

The June air smelled fresh and clean; it was a gorgeous afternoon, and there were still three hours of decent sunlight. Elizabeth unlocked the storage room alongside the basement and got out the shovel, trowel, and her plastic gardening gloves. She liked the way she felt when she had a project of her own like this to focus on, involving some organizing, some "decoration," and some physical activity.

She felt the need of the activity. Events at work this week had made her very uncomfortable. On Tuesday she had accidentally left the bill-of-sale for the new car on the copier (she felt it was wise to keep an original and a copy of important documents). She'd realized it immediately after she'd gotten to her office, but when she went back to the copier the bill-of-sale was gone. She squelched a rising panic reminiscent of grade school, to be "caught" copying personal documents on college time was one thing; to have someone else in the office know how much she had paid for her vehicle was another.

This emotion was followed by rage that someone would actually remove the document from the copier, when they could have put it discreetly to the side, or even returned it to her, but to *take* it? What reason would anyone have to take it but to humiliate her in some way?

"Lydia, do you remember who was last here at the copier?" she had asked the assistant who sat nearest to the machine.

"I think it was Tom."

Tom Murphy.

Elizabeth had gone back to her office to contemplate what she should do next. As she came in she had heard Liz on the phone in the other office. Liz giggled, nervously, said a few indecipherable words and then hung up, glancing up at her for a second as Elizabeth as she closed the door between their offices. Elizabeth had thought her glance looked a bit guilty.

Could Liz have been part of this? Elizabeth had noted how she and Tom were more and more chummy, having lunch once or twice a week in the building's small cafeteria.

On the following day, equally disturbing, she had walked by Lindell's office. He was talking to Tom Murphy, and she caught a phrase through the half-open door: "You know, I've worked with people like her all my life; there's one in every office; she has no *life*...." They had both paused and looked at her through the huge glass window as she walked by, and although neither looked surprised or guilty, who else could they have been talking about?

Later that afternoon she found the bill-of-sale, folded, in her interoffice mailbox. There was no note on it. Was it possible it had been in her box since the previous day? She doubted it; she would have seen it.

In her head, she composed an email to Lindell, copying Tom Murphy, in which she spoke, calmly, of the importance of respect for privacy in office interactions and her mystification at why someone would take private property from a co-worker (not to mention *superior*)... Thinking of this email had taken up most of the day yesterday. She wasn't sure whether to pursue it or not.

Even though she knew he was an idiot, Lindell's comment was crude and hurtful. It wasn't as though she didn't know what others thought of her; she knew that many at the college thought her stiff and formal. But, really, there was no changing that. *You are who you are,* she thought. To *try* and be different was disingenuous. You could improve yourself; you could change certain behaviors, but *you were who you were.* Her mother had said this to Elizabeth and her brother many times when they were growing up, and Elizabeth remembered yelling in exasperation, "Why can't you be who you aren't!" one time when she was a teenager and her mother was particularly annoying. To her recollection, her mother had not responded.

Sometimes Elizabeth had moments of doubt about herself, especially in the past 10 years as she heard of employees whose children were now in college, and other, even younger employees at the college got engaged, and married, and had children. There were a few she admired, who had the skills and organization required to have a professional life and a family. But most just got by, she thought, doing rather shoddy work and finding any excuse to move along on the backs of others.

She had seen Tom Murphy's type many times before on campus: coming from corporate to academia to get a taste of the non-profit world, acting worldly, and moving on before their real ignorance and unwillingness to put in the required work was evident to all. Still, she wasn't sure whether an email, while appropriate (if she could prove he had taken the document), would be effective.

Elizabeth had stopped digging and was sitting cross-legged on the grass, thinking of the email. She looked at her work: this bed along the back fence was almost filled in with eight flats. The delicate purple-and-white flowers looked pretty, dream-like, even in late afternoon shadow.

Something tapped gently at her back and she twisted around. A soccer ball was behind her, and Lucy stood in the middle of the yard with her hand sheepishly over her mouth. "Hello, Lucy. It's okay, it didn't hit me hard. How are you?"

Lucy didn't answer, but uncovered her mouth and smiled slightly, looking down. Elizabeth rolled the ball back to her. Lucy picked it up and kicked it around lightly, staying near the middle of the yard, acting as if Elizabeth wasn't there. Elizabeth watched a while. She appreciated Lucy's shyness. She would've liked to play ball with her, but it felt too awkward to ask. Lucy looked healthy enough, although after seeing her in the window a few weeks before Elizabeth could not help but wonder whether the family was treating her well. Her black hair was tangled and she looked like a ragamuffin in long plaid shorts with her pale thin calves poking out, a long sleeved red T-shirt and baggy red socks with sneakers. The clothing looked like it belonged to someone else, and Elizabeth felt a pang of sadness. If there were a way for her to get a decent wardrobe for this child, she would. It would include clean white T-shirts and khaki skorts for play, and a bright full-skirted dress and patent leather shoes for formal occasions, and maybe even some blue jeans and a knit sweater. And a long flannel nightgown, pale blue, with ripples at the collar and hem, and a matching bathrobe....

She must be tired; she was going off on tangents. She stood up stiffly—she'd been on the ground for almost two hours, she realized—and gathered up her gardening tools. Lucy laughed and said suddenly, pointing at her, "Pants. You wear pants."

"Yes, I wear pants." She smiled. It occurred to her that Lucy had possibly never seen her in any clothes except her suits from work. She took the shovel and trowel back to the storage room, and then made another trip for the remaining unplanted flats. She would go by Home Depot again tomorrow or the next day: she wanted this yard outlined in impatiens. Elizabeth liked the way Lucy followed her, watching. She scooped up some dirt from a bag of potting soil into a small pot from the shelf, tucked a flower in it, and gave it to Lucy.

Lucy smiled. "Papa say you are *å khó ưa*."

"Hmmm. What is that?"

Lucy shrugged.

"Lu-CEE!" Her mother's voice screeched from the backyard. Lucy's face fell. She gave the small flower pot back to Elizabeth and ran off. Perhaps her parents had told her not to accept gifts from strangers. Was she a stranger? She supposed she was. She wondered what Mr. Phan had said she was.

It was dusk now. She felt sad. She wished she had access to a sink, but she wasn't going to bother unlocking the downstairs apartment just to wash her hands. As she got into her car which was parked in front of the building, another large car pulled up behind her. She recognized it from when she and Liz had been by the other week. Three Asian men and one woman got out, carrying bags of groceries. They didn't notice her. Elizabeth watched as one of them fumbled in his pocket for a key to the Phans' apartment and let them all in.

Chapter 29

Reeled In

It wasn't until the beginning of August that she finally decided to speak to Liz about her work, and on that day Elizabeth came in early. The office was empty. She put on a pot of coffee, read her email, and went over her notes. The documentation was in order, and this would just be a warning session. In the past three weeks, Liz had gotten up from her desk an average of ten times a day. To do what? The Ladies Room and lunch could account for three or four times. They hadn't had any major proposals going out so there was no need for much scanning during that time. She'd seen her: in Tom's office, in Ann's office, chatting with Jim Lindell's assistant. Liz was well-liked, and that was a good thing, but this back-and-forth, the secretive phone calls, coming in late (although that didn't bother her so much; she herself had been coming in later and later) was something that simply needed to be reeled in.

To his credit, Lindell had supported her on her email about the sharing of Liz's time. He'd brought it up in the management meeting the day before yesterday, noting that the grants area of Institutional Advancement was a crucial one and that time spent in that department was to be respected. Neither Tom nor Ann nor anyone else said anything in response to it, although she was sure she hadn't improved her relationships with anyone in the room through this memo. That didn't matter. She was not looking for friendship or favors, just respect.

Nevertheless, she was nervous about speaking to Liz. She wanted to be firm but not harsh. She had been reading in a couple of her old management books about timing and approach for disciplinary actions. She had thought about what to wear today, and chosen her gray suit, and had put her hair up. She had every confidence that Liz would recognize the seriousness of the situation and settle down.

Elizabeth heard Liz come in and called out a hello to her; Liz responded in kind. She let her settle in and then went to the doorway.

"Good morning, Liz. When you're settled, could you please come in and see me?"

"Sure." Liz gave her a puzzled look.

When she came in, Elizabeth positioned herself with her notebook at the worktable and offered Liz a chair across from her, smiling. Liz sat down.

"Liz," she began, "You know better than most all the work we have to accomplish in the Grants area." She raised her eyebrows looking for a response and Liz nodded, warily.

"It's detail-oriented and requires a lot of focus."

Liz was looking at her.

"And I feel that some of that focus is definitely eroding. I'm not sure exactly why, but it is." She shifted her papers to pull out the page where she'd marked the times Liz had gotten up from her desk, lined up like tidy fence sections across the pale green grid paper. "I've been keeping a tally of the times you get up from your desk. I'm sure many of these times— maybe even half—are legitimate, but it is obvious to me that you are very distracted...."

"You've been marking down when I get up from my desk?" Liz's voice was incredulous.

"Yes, and I think you yourself would be surprised—"

"I can't believe you've been doing that. I can't believe it!"

"Well, obviously, if your distraction wasn't a serious issue—of course I would not be spending *my* time keeping track of *your* time. I'm simply thinking that if we can acknowledge the situation, the problem—and reel in..."

"'Reel in'? Reel *me* in? Elizabeth, I'm not some kind of *fish*."

"That's not what I meant. You know what I meant." Elizabeth had felt herself go off-kilter for a moment but found her grounding again. "And I think you know what I mean about this lack of focus lately—things left undone, or poorly done...."

They both paused a moment, looking at each other. Liz's gray eyes were angry and full of tears.

"I don't think..." Liz began, then was silent for another few seconds before continuing. "I don't think I can do this, this way." She paused again, swallowing. "I think I need to leave. You can consider this my two weeks' notice."

Elizabeth was startled. "Liz, this is simply a discussion of the seriousness of the situation, not a demand for your resignation."

"I don't think I can work for someone who's marking down *each time I leave my desk*. And, right now, I think I feel sick. I'm going to go home. I'll write you up a resignation letter by tomorrow." Liz stood up awkwardly, almost knocking the chair over behind her.

"Well, that is obviously your decision..."

"Right. *My* decision."

Liz closed the office door quietly behind her, and Elizabeth sat at the worktable until she heard Liz leave. This was not the way she had meant for it to go, not at all. Had she been too harsh? Had it been the wrong thing to do, keeping a tally on Liz? But she could think of no other way to quantify the behavior.

Elizabeth was trying to think straight but couldn't. She knew from previous experience that the best thing to do right now was to get back to work. In the stress of the moment, nothing could be properly figured out. In fact, she wouldn't be surprised if Liz came in tomorrow and had reconsidered. If she left, what would she and Jack do about the missed income, not to mention the health insurance? If she came back, Elizabeth would welcome her reconsideration and not say a word about today's interaction, and they could work on the situation over time. Beyond this, it was best not to think much about it. It would be what it would be. She felt a little better now and pulled out her work for the day: the "Needs" section of Sahil's reapplication to the National Science Foundation.

Chapter 30

A Perfectionist

She was a bit surprised to find Liz already in when she arrived the next day. "Good morning, Liz," she called out, putting her bag down and hanging up her coat.

"Good morning." Liz's voice sounded normal.

Liz's resignation was on her desk, dated, short and to-the-point:

> *To: Elizabeth Wright*
> *From: Elizabeth MacKenzie*
>
> *This is written confirmation that I am resigning my position as Assistant in the Office of Grants effective two weeks from today.*

It was copied to Lindell and to Human Resources.

Elizabeth's heart sank. She decided, quickly, to act as though she hadn't yet seen the memo. "I've got a meeting, and I'm late," she said, putting on her coat again. "I should be back in an hour or so." She made a point of gathering up some file folders, and walked briskly back out to her car (she had to assume Liz was watching out the window) and drove to the main campus, where she found herself having a cup of lukewarm tea in the student cafeteria. She felt she needed to get her mind around the situation, but what was there to comprehend? Liz was an adult; she could make her own decisions. This didn't involve Elizabeth, really. If Liz was so unable to take reasonable critique, then there probably wasn't much future for her in the Grants Office anyway.

Still, she felt sad.

"Well, this is very unusual," she heard Sahil's voice behind her. "May I?" he said, as he sat down next to her with a cup of coffee and two chocolate donuts. "What brings you to the student cafeteria?"

"Liz has given me her resignation."

"Liz, the one who assists you?"

"Yes."

"Why?"

Elizabeth sighed. "It's a long story, but it seems she's not a good fit."

"But she was so excellent, you said so yourself."

"Well, things have changed. Since we moved off campus with everyone else, she's perpetually distracted; her work is going downhill; and when I tried to speak to her about it yesterday she was very defensive." It made Elizabeth feel better to summarize the situation aloud. She decided not to mention the time management log to Sahil.

"Well, that is too bad. Too very bad," Sahil said matter-of-factly, finishing his second donut. "She was the only one you liked since I've been at the college."

"Yes."

"You seem sad," he said.

"Well, I *am* disappointed."

"You are a perfectionist, my friend," Sahil said. "It's very hard to find good help when you are a perfectionist." He patted her hand.

Elizabeth took Sahil's remark as a compliment. He was right. Being particular was her cross to bear. But what should she do—settle for lower standards?

She knew what she would do: she would not try to talk Liz out of her decision. She would make the best use of these final two weeks to get the office in order. She would ask Liz to put together a manual of her tasks, and to give her a full tour of the grants database. And she would place an ad for a new assistant immediately, so that neither Liz nor anyone else would make any assumptions about her being disappointed.

When she got back to the office, Liz had gone to lunch and left a note for her that she had some personal business to take care of and wouldn't be back in for the afternoon. Elizabeth knew that Liz had a day or two of sick time coming but if this continued, she'd have to shut it down immediately. She typed up a list of tasks, including the manual that she wanted Liz to accomplish before she left.

Chapter 31

Exit Interview

Liz's last two weeks at the college were possibly the most excruciating that Elizabeth had experienced in her 20 years at the university. Others in the office took Liz out to lunch, and made no bones about their feeling that something unfair had happened to her, talking loudly as they came by to pick Liz up, keeping her out for over an hour—two hours on two different days—and talking loudly again as they parted ways in the hallway. Elizabeth feigned bright indifference to their behavior, even as she longed to stay home herself until it was all over. Instead, she made a point of being in the office before Liz, and of staying until after Liz left for the day. She and Liz were cordial with each other, and it appeared that Liz was neutrally engaged, not hostile, on the manual of tasks and description of the grants subdirectories.

Lindell had flipped his allegiance, if he'd ever had any, entirely over to Elizabeth, checking in on her a couple of times. "How are things going?" he asked each time.

"Things are under control," she replied. "Did you forward the position announcement to HR?" She knew Lindell understood where his bread was buttered, that if he caused even a slight ripple about this situation with administration, he would be the one having the problem, not her. She had an impeccable record with the school, which would not be disturbed due to the resignation of one assistant who had been at the university for two years.

But Elizabeth went home exhausted each night of those two weeks from having to monitor the situation so tightly.

On Liz's last day, a group of people were taking her out for lunch, and Liz said she would not be back afterward.

"Well, I'm heading out now," Liz said, and extended her hand to Elizabeth. A sudden swell of emotion came over Elizabeth and she put her arms around Liz in an awkward hug.

"Now you're making me feel bad," Liz said, hugging her lightly back, sounding like her old self.

"I do wish you and your family the best," Elizabeth said, her eyes filling with tears. "I know you're in a vulnerable state right now and, Liz, I just believe... I just believe that if outside sources hadn't influenced you, things might have turned out differently."

Liz blinked at her and shook her head slowly. "That's not it; that's not it at all. I think," she said, looking past Elizabeth, "You think you know me, but you don't." Her voice was sad. "And you know what else? No one but you ever calls me Liz. My name is Elizabeth."

Elizabeth blinked, and then Liz was gone. As though she were following her out, Elizabeth could picture Liz going down the back stairs, across the parking lot to her car, starting the engine and driving away, for the last time. Elizabeth stared at the leather blotter on her desk, feeling a small wave of panic rise in her chest. Her throat tightened from holding back tears. Why was this happening? Why was Liz leaving? The office seemed very, very quiet, as though there were no one at all on this floor of the building.

She took a deep breath. It had not been her decision. It was not in her control. It was what it was.

Later that afternoon, Lindell stepped into her office, shutting the door behind him. HR had forwarded him a copy of Liz's exit interview. "I thought you should see it. They only send a copy along when they think there's a pattern," he said, smugly. "*Is* there a pattern?"

He wouldn't know; he hadn't been at the college long enough. Elizabeth looked sourly at Lindell over the top of her reading glasses and didn't answer. When he left, she skimmed quickly: *"I resign at this time because of the eroding relationship with my supervisor, Elizabeth Wright... The job is only a part time job and at full-time it was mostly busywork... She doesn't need an assistant— she needs a friend... she no longer trusted me... she doesn't trust anyone... I had to be a buffer between her and other employees, and I know I sometimes took it on as my role to offset her sternness..."*

Liz must have worked hard to write it, although the comment about needing a friend stung. Elizabeth put it aside. Like those plastic pull-down shades on the windows of an airplane, she felt herself closing up, just a little. *Batten down the hatches,* she thought. She had been right not to trust Liz, as evidenced in this document, which would go nowhere. And she knew no one would say a word to her about it, and in a couple of months—perhaps even in a couple of weeks—it— she—Liz—would be mostly forgotten. It was sad, but that was that, just the way things were.

Chapter 32

The Red Sock

Increasingly, going to Aunt May's place a couple of times each week felt like a chore to Elizabeth, but it had to be done. She was especially concerned since she'd seen the woman and two men let themselves in with a key. How many additional keys had been made? How many extra people were living there, and what was she going to do about it? Usually Elizabeth considered herself able to rally to these kinds of confrontations, but since Liz had resigned she had been very tired. And what if the situation was dangerous? What if the others in the house (whom she felt sure were living there— all of the utility bills had increased) were part of some kind of Asian mafia? Although she had wanted to, Elizabeth hadn't told her mother about seeing the others. Her mother would be even more upset than she was.

She parked in her usual spot in front of the house so they would know she was there. Their car wasn't there, but she suspected there was usually someone in the house. It was starting to cool down a little, finally, in mid-September. Elizabeth went through the side gate and surveyed the backyard. She had mown last week so there was no need to do it today. The grass had filled in where the bird bath had been. (It was now in her garage taking up precious space.) She unwound the hose and set up the sprinkler. She knew it was wasteful, but she liked the lawn green. And she knew that the

Phans wouldn't do anything to keep up the yard. Frankly, she wouldn't want them doing anything. She liked doing the yardwork, and it was good to have an excuse to come over regularly.

Elizabeth looked up at the windows, but there was no sign of activity. It had been the same earlier in the week. The back window was still open, with a fan propped in it. She wondered if the mother-in-law was left alone a lot. What was her name? The Phans had been in the apartment for over nine months now; it seemed she should know the woman's name. Nine months, with the rent late every month except the first. She hadn't seen Lucy much since she gave her the flower pot. Perhaps her mother was keeping her from saying hello. Maybe they had sent her to summer camp, although she doubted that.

A window was slightly ajar on the third-floor apartment; Elizabeth didn't remember that. She decided to go up and take a look. The stairs to the third-floor studio were hot and stuffy. For a Saturday the building was quiet. She unlocked the door. There was a yellow blanket in a pile in the corner of the room and wadded balls of fast food wrappings scattered across the floor. A man's black plastic comb lay on the floor near the blanket.

So others *had* been living here! Elizabeth could feel her heart beating in her throat. She walked briskly across the room to the kitchenette and looked through the cabinets, which were empty. The bathroom had been used, obviously, but wasn't particularly dirty. Perhaps they just ate and slept here and left during the day. But how did they get in? She examined the lock, which appeared normal. Was one of them good at lock-jimmying?

This would not stand, she thought to herself, and repeated: *This will not stand.* She clomped loudly down the stairs to the second floor and knocked firmly on the Phans' door. There was no answer. Elizabeth put her ear up against the door; was that shuffling inside as they pretended not to be home? She knocked louder. Finally, exasperated, she found the second-floor key and unlocked the door.

She had never entered the apartment when the Phans weren't home and so was momentarily disoriented as she looked around the front room and realized the apartment was empty, cleared-out. The only standard furniture they had, the red couch, was gone—as were the mattresses on the floor. The kitchen cupboards held a few half-empty jars of unrecognizable sauces and an old box of cereal. No dishware. It looked like the Phans had been gone for at least a week. The bathroom was dirty, the container of Ajax unopened under the sink. Elizabeth walked through the other rooms, lifting the shades: dusty and empty except for bits of trash and tissues. In the closet she saw the same red sock she had found and left on the porch in the winter. Perhaps Lucy had never worn it again. Perhaps it wasn't even Lucy's sock.

Where had they gone? Why had they snuck out? What would happen to Lucy? Elizabeth felt suddenly exhausted and forlorn, as single and arbitrary as the red sock. If there had been a chair in the place, she would have sat down, but there wasn't. She leaned against the wall with her arms folded. For a while she stared at the black water stain in the center of the room from the birdbath, her mind blank. The perfect circle of the stain gave the room a strange symmetry. Gradually, she came back to herself. At least there was no major damage done. Elizabeth calculated how much money she had lost in unpaid rent, perhaps a couple thousand dollars, the thought of which stung her, but just for a moment. Really, she didn't need the money, even though the rent had been a very good deal. She sighed loudly. She'd had enough of trying to help others out, enough of it all. A slight feeling of relief began to come over her. Now she could just sell the place, get out of it—at a loss or not. Her mother would be upset, but they could work through it by cleaning it up again together. Or not. Maybe just hire someone to do it. These thoughts energized her.

Elizabeth considered calling Marlene, the real estate agent, right away, but decided to wait until she got home and told her mother. She removed the fan, locked the window, and checked all the other windows. It felt good to move around. Then she went to the basement for a broom and dustpan and garbage bags to tidy up. She didn't want to think of the place like it was now. Tomorrow she'd call and arrange to have the locks changed.

Chapter 33

I Guess You Didn't Hear

There were several applications for the assistant's job over the following month, and Elizabeth chose two for interviews, but neither was suitable. She had flashbacks of Charlene and her chatter, and that other girl who had temped for a brief time. It was a unique job, she reiterated to Lindell when he asked, and it might take a while to fill. He'd shrugged. "It's your area."

It certainly *was* her area, and she was glad he'd come to appreciate that. She grew used to the quiet. She sent a memo out to the departments that the Grants Newsletter would be suspended for a while. Other than that, she was able to keep up with the filing and piles of mail herself. After the third unsuccessful interview Elizabeth decided to give herself a break until January. She was tired. She would take a long vacation over the holidays and get back to her former self.

It was Monday evening, a week after Thanksgiving, at the grocery store, that she literally bumped into Liz, their carts tapping as each rounded the corner of an aisle. If she had seen her first, Elizabeth would certainly have avoided an interaction and gone to the other side of the store, but it was too late now.

"Hello," she said awkwardly. Liz looked exhausted, her hair possibly unbrushed, pulled back into an errant ponytail, and dark circles under her eyes. She wore slacks and a sweater, so perhaps she had a new job, or was looking for one. She certainly couldn't interview in that outfit, though, Elizabeth thought.

"Hello." Liz met her look briefly, then gazed over her shoulder down the aisle.

Perhaps leaving the college had sent Liz on a decline, Elizabeth thought. It might have been harder than she thought to find a job when she left so dramatically. "How are you?" she asked.

Liz shrugged. She seemed jumpy, which made Elizabeth feel calm.

"And how's the family? How's Isabel?"

Liz looked sharply at her, almost angrily, then looked away again, as if considering whether or not to respond. "I guess you didn't hear."

"Hear what?"

"She got very sick at the beginning of October." She paused. "It happened very quickly." Liz looked down and leaned into her cart to steer it in the opposite direction.

Elizabeth felt as if someone had kicked her. "Oh my God. Isabel." She had an image of Isabel in her mind, from the birthday celebration in the summer, her soft puffy red cheeks and that exuberant chortle. She was so robust. It didn't seem possible that she could have died. "Oh my God, I'm so sorry! How are you—and Jack—holding up?"

Liz just shrugged and began heading away from Elizabeth down the aisle.

No wonder she looked so bad, Elizabeth thought. No wonder.

"If there's anything I can do…," she called out.

Liz did not respond as she moved away, faster now, leaving Elizabeth standing in the aisle. She hung onto her cart for a few moments to get her bearings. How ironic to find herself in the baby aisle, her vision gradually registering the brightly colored boxes of baby cereal and jars of mashed carrots and green beans. More than once in college Elizabeth had bought jars of banana baby food and ate it like dessert. She loved the just-so sweetness of it and saved the small jars for paperclips and thumbtacks....

Elizabeth realized she was weeping. Other shoppers were beginning to look at her and so she did what she had never done before: she left the store, leaving her half-filled cart in the aisle for some store employee to deal with.

Chapter 34

Like Waves

Elizabeth went to bed when she got home. Her mother had met her at the door, expecting to help unload groceries, but Elizabeth waved her off as she headed up to her room. After an hour or so, Mrs. Wright came up to see what was so upsetting.

"Isabel died." And on seeing she didn't immediately understand, Elizabeth practically yelled at her mother, "*Isabel*, Liz's baby girl. I ran into her in the grocery store and I found out that she got very sick… and died!"

"Oh," her mother frowned. "That's a bad lot." She hesitated, then left Elizabeth alone.

She came up again later. "Do you want some dinner?" she asked.

"No."

At some point Elizabeth took off her suit and put on sweatpants and a sweater. She stayed in bed until late that night, alternately crying and dozing. Other images came to her mind: the infant in the hospital, her tiny, perfect, incomprehensible hands; the baby nursing before Liz handed her off to Jack, when she was still working part-time…. that pink dress she was wearing for Elizabeth's birthday celebration… She thought of Liz's last day—where was Isabel that day? Happily playing at the daycare center. Or maybe she hadn't been happy. Maybe it had been too soon for Isabel to spend long days away from her home.

Had they had medical insurance when Isabel got sick? Did Liz and Jack wait too long to take the baby to the doctor? Perhaps she'd been too hard on Liz. Perhaps she should never have made the assistant's job full-time, as Liz had written in her exit interview. Elizabeth cried and thought these thoughts and let them gather in layers on her like a thick film.

She slept. At some point, probably early in the morning, her mother had come in and hung up her suit which she'd left in a pile on the floor. Elizabeth got up and called Lindell's secretary to say she was sick and wouldn't be in, and it was true she felt so sad that it was almost like being sick. Her body ached all over.

Her mother brought her a bowl of oatmeal and a cup of tea, which Elizabeth appreciated because she was hungry. Mrs. Wright sat on the side of the bed. She was careful with her daughter, having not seen her this way before.

"That's a bad lot," she repeated. When Elizabeth didn't respond she said, "But they have the other child, right? And they can have another baby."

Elizabeth found herself crying again. "That's not the point, Mother."

"I've never seen you this upset."

"Yes, I'm upset. And I'm just going to *be* upset. Thank you for the breakfast; now I'd just like to be left alone." Elizabeth wished she lived alone. She wished she had the house to herself. Why, for instance, was her mother alive, and Isabel dead? The thought came into her mind like a dart; she felt badly about it, but it lingered for most of the afternoon.

She thought of Tom and Ann and the secretaries in the cubicles outside Lindell's office. Had none of them known about the baby's death? Hadn't Liz kept in touch with any of her so-called friends from the college? Had everyone known and kept it from Elizabeth, the not-knowing a further punishment?

Elizabeth watched television in her bed, alternately dozing and gazing aimlessly at the screen. When she muted the sound, she felt a wave of sorrow rise up like a wave and slide over her—it was just like they said, grief—just like water, like waves.

Another day and another passed. She didn't get dressed. It snowed an inch. She heard her mother outside shoveling the driveway. After she called in sick on Friday morning, Mrs. Wright brought her breakfast and said from the doorway, "You know, Elizabeth, this is getting to be too much. It's self-pity. Why are you feeling sorry for yourself? It was *her* baby that died. There was nothing you could do about it. So you may as well get out of bed."

She stayed in bed all day, but her mother's words had sunk in and Elizabeth knew she was right. In the late afternoon, tired and hungry and empty, she got up and took a shower and ate the lamb chops Mrs. Wright had prepared.

Chapter 35

A Grieving Process

Elizabeth had to drag herself to work on Monday. It was the first time in several years she had felt so profoundly apathetic; it almost frightened her. It's a grieving process, she told herself. You're *grieving*. She deserved a few sick days to take it all in. When she got to the office, she'd look up "Grief" on the internet. That might help her focus and get back on track.

She also decided to wear slacks. It was still a suit, but she couldn't bear the thought of pantyhose that day. Lydia smiled at her sympathetically when she arrived, "How are you feeling, Elizabeth?"

"Better, thank you." Elizabeth did not pause as she went by.

"I've never seen you in pants! They look great," she added.

One thing she knew she needed to do, much as she didn't want to, was speak to Tom Murphy about Liz's baby. Had he known? If he didn't, then the news would probably be a shock to him, too. It would also mean he and Liz had not been as friendly as she had supposed. If he had known and didn't tell her....

Elizabeth turned on her computer and turned up the thermostat in her office. Her mail was stacked in two haphazard piles on her desk. She skimmed through her email. Other than a couple from Sahil, everything was either spam, campus notices, or grantsmanship updates. She felt exhausted. Maybe she *was* getting sick.

She was unable to focus all morning. She needed a real vacation, she thought, but the idea did not lead into any of her usual daydreams of cruises or road trips. At midday there was a brief knock and the door opened before she could respond. Tom Murphy stood awkwardly in the entry and they looked at each other for a moment, mutually surprised. Elizabeth could see he hadn't expected her to be in.

"Uh, Elizabeth," he said. "I heard you were out, and… came to see how you were."

"I doubt that," she said.

He laughed. "Okay, caught. I was going to use your view of the parking lot to see whether Ann had left yet or not."

"Be my guest." She felt so tired that she knew she'd have to go home. It was no use.

"Tom," she said as he was about to leave. "Do you hear from Liz—er—Elizabeth?" she asked. Her own name felt strange on her tongue. She felt herself flush, revealed, but Tom didn't seem to notice.

"She's doing very well. Got another job, at the *Gazette,* editing press releases. They're already talking about having her write, too." His voice was proud, rubbing in his friendship with Liz.

"But what about Isabel?" Elizabeth pretended to be looking through the mail.

"She's good. She was pretty sick a few weeks ago—they had to take her to the emergency room and do some tests— but it was just a really bad viral thing."

"She's… okay?"

"Well, yeah. Elizabeth said it was pretty scary, but Isabel's okay. That kid's really something, she's a real trooper."

Tom stood awkwardly in the doorway until Elizabeth dismissed him with a forced smile. She got up and closed the door softly behind him and sat back down at her desk, blinking. *A real trooper:* her mind was stuck on the phrase. *Isabel was not dead.* There was a sense of having woken up from a bad dream, a delirium. She had been lied-to. Elizabeth carefully scanned her memory of the afternoon at the market. Hadn't Liz's cart had several jars of baby food in it? Hadn't she refused to look at Elizabeth, averting her gaze the entire conversation?

Had Liz actually said the baby had died?

Elizabeth couldn't remember, exactly. If she had come in to the office that next day she could have simply asked Tom, as she had just done, and the whole rest of the week wouldn't have been... lost... badly, sadly spent. She thought of all she had been through, thinking of that baby—that baby who was and would remain totally and completely oblivious of Elizabeth's existence... Had Liz intended to confuse her? How could Liz be so angry at her? It was mind-boggling. Was she unstable? Did Jack know what she had done?

Perhaps she should call him.

Elizabeth was glad the baby was alive, but somehow she did not feel better; a grief was not alleviated. She had been sitting at her desk for over an hour. Gradually, slowly, the objects in her office were coming into focus: the coat stand, the rows of books (mostly old and available online now), the horizontal file drawer with a stack of files piled on it and the plastic undecorated Christmas tree that she'd just pulled out last week, the empty work table, her desk in front of her.

Except for the clock she received last year, with a small engraved tab recognizing her for 20 years of service to the college, the office could have belonged to anyone—anyone at all.

She needed to call her mother and let her know what had transpired. She could already imagine her response, "Well, I can't imagine. I can't imagine; that's a strange lot, a very strange lot," and she'd make Elizabeth tell her about it again and again until she could form a conclusion. Sahil would say something similar.

This little interlude would pass. She was old enough to know that. Finally, it would be like nothing at all. Something that had happened and passed. Sitting there, Elizabeth saw how it could all go—how it probably *would* all go—perhaps retiring early, redoing the kitchen like they'd planned, taking a trip—perhaps a tour to Rome, although, really, she didn't have an interest in going to Rome—her mother's demise, living in the house alone....it all lay before Elizabeth as clear and predictable—and sad—as… as anything. She knew she would snap out of it; one had to, after all, but for these minutes now she just sat looking out the large office windows at the overcast sky. Autumn had come and gone quickly this year. It would be Thanksgiving again soon. The branches on the trees on the other side of the parking lot were almost bare, swaying in some wind. Elizabeth watched a small gust take the last of the leaves up into the air, suspended for a moment before they scattered on the smooth black pavement.

About the Author

Virginia Weir grew up in the Southwest, graduated from San Francisco State University, and completed an MFA in fiction from Warren Wilson College. Throughout a life of writing, she has worked as a typesetter, database administrator, grant writer, and fundraiser. She lives with her husband in Connecticut. www.VirginiaWeir.com